TWO BODIES

MASSIMO PARADISO

First published in 2024 by Eyes & Teas.

Print ISBN: 978-1-7393941-1-0

Ebook ISBN: 978-1-7393941-0-3

A CIP record for this book is available from the British Library.

For Emilie

BOOKS BY MASSIMO PARADISO

After Arrival

Lucky's Woods

Two Bodies

'Pissing, bloody, potholes!' Caz Turner said, as her little car bounced down the road. She looked into her rear-view mirror but her view was blocked by the immense load of wood she had squeezed into her boot that morning.

'Oh yeah,' she said to herself. 'Forgot you were in there, weighing down my poor little car.' She caught her face briefly in the mirror before returning her gaze to the road, she should have put a beanie on. She'd had a battle with the elements that morning. It was a clear but windy day in Furlong, Sussex. Blue skies were painted above the town while the low hanging sun cast shadows far and long. Caz had struggled to hold onto the planks of wood from their old rotting shed as she brought them out to the car one by one. It was almost as if they had invisible hands that grasped at the wind as it tore by. After a couple of fly-away pieces, and a third splinter, Caz donned some gardening gloves and finally wrestled the entire shed into the back of her little hatchback, snapping a few rotten pieces here and there to aid with the task. It was one hell of a wakeup call. The wind had also got hold of her hair and thrown it in all directions. Caz was now on her way to the tip to drop off her load and then hopefully get back home in time to start work at nine a.m.

Caz worked as a new business manager for a London design agency. She worked remotely and her start time was a little foggy to say the least, as was her finishing time, but she tried to keep a routine. The mornings were mainly for chores, if she'd dragged herself out of bed. Sometimes she'd wake to find it was gone ten, meaning her husband, Adrian Hoarding, had managed to complete his entire morning routine and leave without waking her. She wasn't jealous of his office based job in nearby Brighton, but she did miss his goodbyes.

Caz always got an immense sense of satisfaction going down the tip and getting rid of crap. It was both therapeutic and liberating. Not only that, she enjoyed the organisation of the system; the questions at the gate, the bay she was assigned, the process of unloading, the colour coded system, the rotation of containers. It was all oddly calming despite the noise from the trucks and the squawking gulls trying their luck at a few remaining pieces. She stopped at a set of traffic lights and clicked open the glove compartment in search of a hair band. She kept one eye on the lights as she rummaged around but unfortunately came up empty handed. The red of the lights held steady so she searched the rest of the car and managed to find one behind the seat. It looked more than a little worse for wear and the springiness had faded like a broken accordion. She slipped it on to her wrist, quickly pulled her hair together in a haphazard bun, then wove it tighter. She gave it a little jiggle for structural integrity; it seemed to do the job. She snapped the glove compartment shut just as the amber light blinked on and she pulled off again, eyeing up a car on the left that looked as if it fancied running a red light in the other direction. The disgruntled man caught her eyes and brought the car to a hasty stop, his body lurching forward wanting to get to wherever he was going.

On arrival at the tip, Caz was glad to see she didn't have to queue. She slowly pulled up to the booth where a man was sitting in his high vis jacket reading a paper.

'Morning luv,' he said in a chirpy tone. The "luv" grated her but she let it go. The man was part of her favourite system, after all.

'Hiya. Just wood,' she said. 'Our old shed'. She knew the ropes.

'Blimey. You've done well to fit all that in there ain't ya? Bay eight will do you.' He pointed in the direction of all the bays. 'Right opposite the wood for you.'

'Cheers.' She waved her thanks and rolled off to the bays, reversing back into the empty space with a crisp white figure eight painted on the ground. She waited for the soft bump to come against her wheel, then killed the engine. She reached up to secure her makeshift bun which had begun to slip. She tightened it, then stepped out into the crisp morning.

Caz made her way to the back of the car. Sure enough, gulls circled above eyeing up the spoils of wasteful humans while the brown sign saying 'wood' wobbled merrily on its metal post as the gusts came and went. The wind was a little calmer than it had been at her house, which was just a road away from the seafront promenade and the English Channel. The local tip was located at the foot of the South Downs which allowed the majority of the town's buildings to take the edge off. She cast her eyes up to the hills as her boot yawned open. She knew from experience that anyone who happened to be at the top of the downs today would be getting the full force of the South-Westerly's.

Although their bodies lived in town, Adrian and Caz's hearts lived in the South Downs. They were the ones that beat down the grasses on paths less trodden, saw the surprisingly vast landscapes and talked to the grazing animals. At times it felt like a private museum that was all theirs to enjoy. Caz often wished the rest of the world was equally empty. She unwittingly kept herself up some nights playing out post-apocalyptic scenarios. First off to the Cable's Wood gun club to arm up, then a supermarket sweep in whatever SUV she had "borrowed".

Caz donned her gardening gloves that she'd left in the boot and began by gathering three planks to see how she would fare against the wind. The first couple of trips went well, each ending with a satisfying clunk at the bottom of the recently emptied wood container. She then hauled out a larger piece. Knowing it would certainly fancy a free ride on the wind, she waited for her moment. She loved a little game, it made even the most mundane tasks fun. The wind carried over a male voice on one of its gusts.

'Oh bugger.'

Looking to her right, Caz saw an old man scrambling around the aftermath of a failed deposit of tree branches into the garden waste container. Luckily, one of the centre staff was quick to respond and headed over. The car sighed a little as she lifted the panel up in the next break of wind. She'd forgotten how heavy it was. Pinning it in the bend of her waist she rotated and squatted across to the container, leaned back to get the panel onto the lip, and readjusted her grip. She saw a high-vis jacket approaching in her peripherals, and guessed one of the staff might have seen a damsel who needed relief from some distress. Caz gritted her teeth and snapped her legs straight, sending the panel crashing into the container. She gave her hands the perfunctory brush of a job well done and looked down the line of containers to the worker who had stopped in his tracks. He gave a nod which conveyed both admiration and understanding and went back to cleaning up the last of the tree branches. Caz blew a stray clump of hair from her face and nodded back.

It was a hazard-free trip on the whole. She rolled up the tarp lining her car boot and raised the rear seats back into place. The day was now hers, her work day being as busy as she chose it to be, it was only a Monday after all. Adrian wouldn't be home until later that night - he was going climbing. Starting up the engine, she already felt the satisfaction of a successful trip to the tip creep in.

'God,' she groaned. 'You need to get a proper hobby, *luv*'.

Mona Turner hung up the call to her sister and chucked the phone back in her desk drawer. She did envy Caz's ability to work from home at hours of her choosing, and on the days of her choosing. Not Mona. She was stuck, willingly, to the clockwork life of a teacher. She taught in the local secondary school. She had no choice in the matter when it came to starting times or breaks. But Mona only really envied Caz during term time. It wasn't a problem when she was on a school break. Alas, swings and roundabouts.

Chatter in the hall told Mona most of the pupils had arrived. She looked at the municipal clock hanging above the window – still a couple of minutes to spare. She opened the drawer and took her phone out again. She was trying to buy a property – her first one. The process hadn't really started in earnest though because she just couldn't find anything she liked. Was she being too picky? Absolutely. Did she also spend a bit too much time adjusting the filters so she could nose into the bigger properties and scoff at their hideous interiors? Absobloody-lutley. She'd just put some criteria into the filters when a scream cut through the babble from the corridor outside. Mona gave it another moment, her thumb hovering over the phone's screen.

'Justin! I'm going to fucking kill you. Eerrrrrrrraaaaaaa!' Mona took the expletives as meaning enough to go and police the situation. If Justin was involved, Mona already had a good idea who owned that shrieking voice.

She pulled the door open and popped her head out, and was met with the same sight anyone teaching teenagers would likely see across the U.K. Right beside the door were her star pupils, the boys wearing ties in double Windsors, and the girls wearing skirts the agreed school length. They greeted her with warm smiles, eye rolling at the immature behaviour behind them. Then came the bread and butter students; a mismatch of ruffled hair, novice makeup skills and some vacant stares which housed fairly competent brains. A few were enjoying the scene unfolding just down the corridor, others using the brief window to check their phones. Then, at the back of the pubescent hormone conga line: the wild ones. It was always hard to pin down how many could be found in this section in any one day. Situations changed regularly for these individuals, by no fault of their own in most cases. This group was actually Mona's favourite. They showed a zest for life, knew how to throw a witty retort and needed the most attention. They also required some acknowledgement of their worth from teachers to show they were human beings and the system wasn't leaving them behind. This is where Mona found Justin, and as predicted, his current love interest, Priya.

'Oh, chill out,' Justin said. 'It's only a few hairs.'

'Yes Justin, *my* hairs. Not yours to fucking hack away at!' Priya replied. Her many years of teaching had taught her to have a very unbiased view of "student situations" until she had all the pieces of a puzzle.

'Priya,' Mona said, loudly but calmly down the hall. 'Language.'

'Miss, he just snipped my *bloody* hair!'

Usually, Mona would ask Justin if this was true, but the throng of students had parted, giving Mona a better view. She was greeted with pieces of the puzzle, and it was quite a big piece. In one hand, Justin held a pair of round edged school issue scissors, dotted with paint from the art and crafts studio, and the other hand didn't hold "only a few hairs" as he claimed, but a handful of Priya's dark glossy hair. Enough to attach to a couple of toy dolls and send them off to a tea party.

Mona made straight for Justin. His stupid smirk fell from his face with each step Mona took towards him. By the time Mona arrived in front of him, he had his hands outstretched with both pieces of evidence, and his head bowed. He looked like a slug surrounded by salt. Mona carefully plucked the scissors and hair from his hand and turned to face Priya. Her eyes had filled with tears and it looked as if she was straining to suck them back in. Mona quickly weighed up her options. Justin had definitely gone too far. Mona quickly spun the scissors around, tightly grasping the blades, and offered the handle to Priya.

'Time for you to take a chunk off his mop, I think?' Mona smiled. Priya released the tension in her body with a huff.

'Miss…'

'Would you like to go to the bathroom, Priya?'

'No, Miss.' Another act of strength to show Justin she was strong, and Priya was strong. Mona had met her foster parents at several parents evenings and was always sure to champion her. Parentless well before she should be, and trying to carry the weight alone for her younger sister, Mona saw a lot of her sister Caz in her. They had lost their parents a bit later, when they were in their mid-twenties, but the sting had been just as fatal. Mona had mourned but Caz - Mona wasn't entirely sure if she ever had. She had gone on to organise the funeral, the estate and plenty more that Mona had never known the true extent of. She had protected Mona from it all and continued to protect her to this day. Caz hadn't been despondent, she'd been there for Mona, but she'd have her little blow ups here and there. Much like Priya, Caz could be unseen unless provoked.

'Head on in. I'll deal with this.' Mona gave her a comforting smile to see her off, then waited for the door to close before rounding on Justin.

'Detention.'

'Yes, Miss,' Justin said to Mona's feet.

'And I will have to report this, Justin. It's abusive behaviour, even though it was meant... You can't go around brandishing scissors, and you certainly can't use them on other students.'

'But it was only–' Justin's head snapped up to defend himself.

'Even their hair, Justin. I shouldn't need to tell you what could have happened if Priya had spun around suddenly.' Mona let the act play out in Justin's consequence free head and saw the revelation land. He returned his gaze to the floor. The incident had clearly happened under the influence of cupid's arrow, but Mona knew Justin couldn't take many more hits like this on his record. She decided to have him sit alone in class for now while she pondered the situation. Justin needed a hand out, not a hand slap.

3

Adrian Hoarding strained his eyes against the harsh light of his phone, which was pinned to his windscreen showing the route to his destination. It said he had two minutes to go until he arrived at Marsh Avenue, Cable's Wood. At present, there were nothing but vacant fields either side of him. He continued deeper into the South Downs.

He couldn't remember the last time he'd been to the isolated hamlet - his country rambles with Caz never came this way. Cable's Wood lay on the outskirts of Furlong and there was no reason to be here unless you knew someone, or wanted to feel unwelcome in a pub. In the two pubs of Cable's Wood, it was common to hear the locals declare Cable's Wood a sovereign state, nothing to do with Furlong, thank you very much. Whereas, on the other side of the coin, Furlong residents considered Cable's Wood just another part of town, which, geographically, it was. They could also be heard mumbling "snobs".

The timer on the display dropped to one minute just as some houses came into view. Adrian's heart rate rose a little as he pulled into a rural street, the tarmac giving way here and there to loose rubble. Cable's Wood didn't have any street lights and this only added to the difficulty of navigating with his phone.

'Bloody thing,' Adrian said as he snatched the phone from the windscreen holder. He stopped the car feeling curtains twitch either side of him.

'Second right.' He clicked the phone off and tossed it on the passenger seat. He continued up the street finding it easier going without the phone's light in his face. He turned into Marsh Avenue a minute later. His headlights revealed a better maintained street; on either side were bungalows, modern with expensive cars neatly parked out front; chalets, with even more polish; and one beautiful, out of place, building. It looked like a large old generator or waterworks building, but it had been converted into a trendy "Grand Design" residence. A warm glow issued from its slither thin windows, but it seemed to be masquerading among the cosy street. That said, it shared the same neatly manicured patch of grass, just outside the front gardens, which meant the houses were set far back. Adrian nodded in approval of this; he didn't necessarily want to be seen. He saw a space near the renovated house and pulled in, then killed the engine. He became immediately aware of his thumping heart.

'Christ. It's quiet up here.' He ducked down to get a better view of some of the houses in the low light.

Very nice.

He picked up his phone and checked his messages. He felt a bit better when he saw one from his colleague, Michael.

'Hey mate, I'm already here. 84, Marsh Avenue. Knock, doorbell is broken.'

Adrian's heart relaxed a little. He wasn't overly worried - he was in Cable's Wood don't you know - but he had never been into a drug dealer's house before.

Michael had assured him there was nothing to worry about. "He's basically family." Michael had said. Adrian wasn't *into* drugs, but he didn't necessarily have a problem with them either. He saw this as a purely medicinal solution to a growing problem.

Adrian had always had a touch of obsessive compulsive disorder, the kind flippantly mentioned when something was out of place. Since he'd tipped over the age of forty, things had got worse. Once amusing habits had become a nuisance - unable to leave the front room until the dimmer was wound back, forth, then set at centre; walking back to the car three times to check the driver, boot and passenger doors. Caz had let a certain amount go, trying to make light of them also - calling his compulsions his "dances", but now it was affecting their relationship.

Caz was always moving forward, Adrian had become stuck in a rut. She detested this. Perhaps more detrimental was his bedtime routine. It now took him a good two hours to get to bed after his various hygienic dances and that left little opportunity for sex. He wished he could get straight into bed, but he felt the dirt of the day on him. It weighed him down. The lack of intimacy ground away at them both. He might lose his mind one day, but he never wanted to lose Caz.

He knew the combined time of all his dances was adding up and that also frustrated him. It was time he'd never get back. The doctors had poked and prodded. It was conclusive, based on behavioural assessment. Then he was given some leaflets and sent on his way. He'd given therapy a shot. He knew it would get worse - there was a fuse burning away inside and he couldn't cut it. Caz had often suggested his work might be part of the issue.

Adrian worked in data analysis, always had, and looked destined to always be. He had an eye for detail, patterns and trends. It used to excite him. But as the data came and went, he became dissatisfied with the industry, jumping from agency to agency around London trying to find that early buzz. He'd been offered his current job, which was based in Brighton, by one of his old bosses. While it was the same work it promised a release from the claws London had him in. Caz had always been desperate to move back to Sussex, and they had planned to start a family - something that was currently alluding them. Adrian couldn't pinpoint why these compulsions had started, but he saw Caz's point: work was repetitive, so were his habits.

A few weeks ago, Adrian stumbled across a documentary on psilocybin, an active chemical inside magic mushrooms, and on further reading thought there might be something in it for him. Unfortunately, he was unable to ask his local pharmacy for it, being a class-A substance and all that. Who knew mushies were a gateway?

Not me, officer. No sir.

He typed a quick reply letting Michael know he'd be there in five, and went to put the phone in his pocket, but hesitated as his OCD began to itch. He couldn't shake the fact he was going into a drug dealer's house, so feeling rather exposed, he checked the time once more, popped his phone in the glove compartment, and just took his keys and wallet.

Adrian stepped out into the cold evening air. It had just turned ten minutes past six in the evening. Caz didn't expect him home until late because he'd said he was going climbing. He wasn't entirely sure why he had lied to her – she would likely be on board with anything that helped the situation. He locked the car and began his dance. On his final return to the car he hesitated a moment with his hand on his back pocket, feeling for his wallet. He whipped it out, removed the eighty pounds he'd specifically taken out in cash, then popped his wallet into the glove compartment with his phone.

'There,' he said, 'now they'll never find you after the dealer slits your throat.'

He locked the door, did his dance all over again, then walked up the street. Although he was nervous about the forthcoming transaction, he couldn't help but feel some old forgotten teenage excitement in his gut. He smiled to himself as he made out the property numbers in the dim light, unaware of the events occurring inside the houses he passed. The silence was nice. Not so silent it pierced the eardrums and brought ringing into the ear canals. More a delicate symphony with the volume turned down low. Off in the distance was the faint whoosh of the A-road that skimmed the outskirts of Furlong. The sound carried in on the wind, and became entwined with the brush of nearby conifers swaying in the breeze. It was punctuated every so often with the staccato tweets of songbirds that still had some song left in them as the day drew to a close. Nearer was the unmistakable hum of electricity from overhead cables that could ruin the look of a single hamlet with one broad stroke. Adrian wondered if they were once fed by the property he had parked outside. Adrian turned to look back down the street. He wasn't doing anything illegal – yet – but was trying to act relaxed like he belonged.

Round the bend, he was greeted with more bungalows, but they were a little different – a lot smaller, and squished together in terraces. The road had widened, removing the grass out front and bringing the houses forward. It didn't feel as private all of a sudden, and Adrian tried to make himself smaller as he walked down the street. Finally, he reached number 84. It was one of the mid-terraced bungalows, even less private. He walked down the short garden path and checked over his shoulder once more, less naturally this time. He started to feel a little hot, even out here in this cold. He moved around in his jacket as he approached the door, trying to shuffle in some cold air.

The entrance looked inviting enough. A stencilled number 84 was shining light through a pane of glass above the door, and a few potted plants with snowdrops and cyclamen showed off their last winter flowers making all the annuals blush their twigs in embarrassment. Adrian knocked as politely as he could so as not to attract any prying eyes from the neighbours. The rap came off a little louder than he would have liked. Adrian's stomach was really bumbling now and he wasn't all too sure if it was due to the nerves or perhaps something else. His thoughts were interrupted by the sound of well-maintained metal bolts being dislodged, and soon he was face to face with someone that he didn't plan to tell anyone about. A drug dealer.

4

Teddy Coren was on his knees, stunned and sobbing with a lifeless body in his arms. A body that was only moments ago alive. Teddy's cool grey eyes were already ringed with puffy red lids as he checked the body up and down, foolishly looking for signs of life. The pulse was gone. But, maybe pulses weren't a thing in this world, he hypothesised? Perhaps human arteries had thicker walls, so as not to give away the secrets of the heart?

Stop being romantic! The scientific side of Teddy shut himself down. *It's not called a parallel universe for nothing. Check his breathing!*

'Yes. Most organisms respire in some manner; even plants breathe.' He pulled the limp, heavy head gently up to his and lightly pressed his ear to the mouth and nose, Teddy quickly pulled away.

'Cold. Why so cold already?'

Strange indeed, echoed the scientist.

'But we've just arrived!' Teddy said. 'We only just came through, what the fuck is going on!' He placed his ear to the cold mouth again, shuddering lightly at the metallic like chill that sucked the warmth from his ear. Teddy held still for a few moments, dead silent, waiting for even the slightest flow of air to reassure him, but there was nothing.

'Oh, Adrian,' Teddy said. He closed his eyes and began to sob, with deep clutching breaths, sporadic, gasping. He felt his head begin to rise, the pressure rising in his head, as if it was being pumped full of helium. It felt like an escape, maybe he would just park himself up here for a while. A whistling began, pushing his head even higher. Then a thud nearby brought Teddy back into the room.

'The bridge!'

He looked around like a feral creature caught off guard, but didn't see anything. He didn't *feel* anything either. The bridge must have collapsed after their arrival. This realisation snapped him out of his despair and he suddenly realised all the TVs had gone, he spun around and took in the rest of the room. It was the same space, but it wasn't his room.

'Oh shit, fuck, shit.' He clawed at his head. 'Fuck.'

Teddy had set up his experiment in a vacant building he was a live-in guardian of in his world. It was an old electrical generator store that had the bare minimum of amenities; a wet room and a freestanding kitchen. But here, it was all different. His floor, which was a carpet of wires, tools and equations was replaced with polished parquet. He carefully laid Adrian's head down and ran to the single, giant TV on the wall, braced himself and pushed the screen. Nothing.

'Fuck.'

This had been a possibility, but the fear still smothered

Teddy in an instant. He was stuck here - on another world. This was someone else's property, and it looked like they'd made it a *home*.

'Or is this mine?'

He was torn between his emotions and the job he had to do. This was *a* living room. Teddy walked over to a sideboard that was pushed up against the wall where his mattress should have been and picked up two photo frames. He tried to blink the tears away and focus on the pictures. They featured a family of three smiling happily in a selfie shot, and none of them were him.

'This... this isn't my house.' Teddy said to himself. A tinge of intrigue now entered his muddled thoughts. 'I don't live here? Where am I?' He was unsure whether he meant this as a question or statement. No matter, they had prepared for this.

Teddy began to execute the process they had agreed in such a situation. Trying not to think about Adrian, Teddy looked towards the back of the room with misty eyes and let his scientific mind take over. The original steel door had been replaced with bi-folds - revealing a well-kept garden.

Good. Identical orientation.

He looked to the opposite wall, at a garish mirrored clock shaped like a night star. Teddy forgot about the clock and just registered the time: 19:12 p.m.

'We didn't lose any time. Extraordinary.'

He felt giddy for the first time since stepping through the bridge. He looked back to Adrian, eager to discuss this, but in his scientific excitement he had already forgotten the horror that had befallen them on their maiden voyage. He felt like his head would explode from the speed his thoughts were running at. He could barely believe they'd actually done it, yet at the same time, he was undergoing the greatest loss of his life. Before he could let the horror fill him once more, a series of thuds brought his senses back.

Those are car doors!

He heard some muffled conversation and shortly after, the jingling of keys. Whoever lived in this house had returned. Teddy ran over to Adrian. He got a good grip under Adrian's armpits and tried to drag him but Adrian barely budged – only enough to become dislodged from the awkward heap he lay in. Teddy was well past "getting on a bit" and not built for physical excursion. His brain was the athlete. Adrian weighed around fifteen stone, and was a dead– Teddy stopped his train of thought. Not dead, limp.

The scientific part of Teddy that had already declared time of death on Adrian, knew what he must do the moment he first saw the body crumpled in a heap on the ground. He had to let go. Physically, now. Emotionally, he didn't know when. Adrian stood a better chance of survival under the care of local authorities the homeowners would no doubt immediately dial in a panic. Teddy couldn't take Adrian anywhere, even if he could carry him. There'd be too many questions.

He looked down at Adrian and let everything fall away for just a few more seconds, pushing his time. Teddy had always heard people say the dead looked 'peaceful', but Adrian just looked uncomfortable. Teddy carefully removed Adrian's rucksack, picked up the mobile which had been documenting the crossing, then checked and emptied his pockets. The police would have a hard time identifying him, but the paramedics would help regardless. Teddy took a deep breath in, closed his eyes and placed a delicate kiss on Adrian's forehead. The sound of talking became louder as the seal around the front door gave way. Teddy pulled himself away, but it felt as if he was leaving a piece of himself behind. He moved to the back doors silently while he heard the chimes of an alarm being disengaged. He slowly turned the key that was already in the barrel, took it and waited, listening to the talking that hung outside in the hallway.

'Get the door behind me would you? Keep that cold out,' said a male voice with a northern accent. Hopefully, the sight of a man lying on their living room floor won't cause any heart attacks or more trouble. Teddy pushed at the same moment he heard the front door slam shut. He stepped out into the garden and began making his way to the right sticking close to the wall. He didn't give in to a final glance – the cold air had knocked some sense into him and he knew he needed to make himself scarce. Teddy continued to the end of the house where a sheltered path made its way to a back gate.

He slipped a hand into his pocket as he walked. He extracted a ring of keys and located one with a number two carved into it. He steeled himself for a moment. The padlock looked the same, so he put the key into it. It slipped in unhindered. He turned it clockwise. The bolt released and so did a breath of relief from Teddy. He spared himself the gloating and quickly slipped the padlock off the gate and placed it in clear view, as if someone had simply forgotten to lock it in the first place.

He poked his head out and quickly checked the familiar alley, clear. Without hesitating, he pulled himself to the right, which led to a lane. He moved Adrian's bag to his chest, keeping his own on his back and pulled his mobile phone out. It had turned itself off.

Odd.

He wanted to seem as natural as possible and started tapping away regardless. Teddy was only two houses down when he heard the first scream from behind him. It sounded childlike. He felt a pang in his gut, but he wrestled it still.

The sirens will start soon. They will help.

He picked up the pace as the lane met an A road which led to Cable's Wood Parade and eventually, Furlong. Brake lights created a red mist ahead as the traffic slowed, it looked like he was approaching the gates of hell. Maybe that's where I'll end up, he thought. He slowed his pace and took it in.

Stricken with shock, he hadn't really had a chance to take in what they'd done, what they'd achieved. It was exactly the same, but it was beautiful. As if all the colours had been amplified, the air made sweeter, the noises crisper, as if he'd been stuck in a dark cave for months on end. Was it just his imagination, or were his surroundings operating on a slightly different frequency that he wasn't yet attuned to?

Were they the first? Was *he* the first to survive? Something had been drastically miscalculated but he didn't have the time to dwell now. He knew he would though, and hard. He had to use the last of the adrenaline to get him to a safe spot where he was already planning his breakdown. He would let his emotions swarm him, consume him, like baby spiders devouring their mother. Oddly, he was looking forward to it, diving into that abyss.

Teddy had often obsessed about losing Adrian and what it might mean for him. At the moment, it didn't really feel like anything had happened. The scientist in him once again took the reins and carried him the final miles to Furlong. They had planned to stay the night at 33 Marsh Avenue, which was meant to be owned by this world's version of Teddy Coren. He had been rather looking forward to that encounter, to see the stunned look on his own face as he stepped through the TV. Teddy had hoped his other self would have been watching the TV as he did so. He had a hotel in mind, if it existed here, but he would be alone.

5

'That'll do,' Kim Chowdry sang to herself as she called it quits. She stretched her arms overhead and looked up from her paperwork, her eyes tired and slow to adjust their focus. The second floor of the Sussex Police building was still a hive of activity despite it being almost eight p.m. People were busy with calls and crisis meetings. Just another day in the office.

Kim had been in a rush to get off today, but it hadn't gone to plan. She was at the end of her four-day shift, which had contained lots of late nights. She looked around and clocked a uniformed officer talking to someone out of view in the main corridor. He seemed to be flirting from the way he smouldered. Kim looked back down at her work. Her laptop whining under all the sheets of paper, the internal fans clawing for more air. She looked at it pitifully for a few seconds, then collected the loose bits of paper covering the keyboard area. The fans gave an audible rev as the suction changed.

Whoops.

Kim worked in the Murder Investigation Team, or MIT for short. Unfortunately, due to some recent cuts, that also covered adolescent murders. Last year there were forty five victims of homicides aged under sixteen. She currently had one adolescent case going through her department and she was leading. She looked through her papers again. Some of these cases would soon end up in the archives of unsolved investigations. Initially, she found these cases hard going, with each investigation carrying its own morbid story. Why on earth was she torturing herself when there was no justice? Kim had nearly quit: but then she got some justice.

His name was Arthur. He was only eight years old. He had hair like hay hanging over big green eyes. She'd never forget those dead eyes. Wide. So wide you'd think he was still alive. A far cry from the eyes in the press photos that squinted with joy as he held up his first ever catch while out crabbing with his family. "Arthur with a Common Shore Crab, 27cm, Shoreham Harbour," said the article. Kim remembered this easily because the crab dwarfed little Arthur's hands.

Unlike most of the cases that came through, Arthur had been lucky enough to have a perfectly average upbringing in his short life. A happy kid with a seemingly loving family. He was simply in the wrong place at the wrong time. She hoped then, as she did most days, that those eight years of love were enough to combat the horrors he had faced during his thirty-six hours of abduction. When she heard the suspect's name being announced as guilty in the stands, a tsunami of emotion drowned her - justice. She saw the release on Arthur's parents' faces as they heard the verdict. The last parts of them clinging onto Arthur's memory, the part selfishly not wanting to let go, snapping free. Justice carrying off the memory to rest in peace. Justice was a complex emotion, but a satisfying one.

Prior to working on murder cases, she had done some time on the street, but only briefly because she'd already done a stint in other public services followed by a detective grad scheme. She'd seen her share of shit, wasted her time on minor indiscretions. Then, after a few internal bumps, government cuts and a lot of hard work, she slipped out of her uniform and into a suit. She liked the fit.

Kim stacked the last mug from the day onto the now embarrassingly high pile, slung her bag over her shoulder and turned to leave. She made it a few desks down when her desk phone let a string of digital saxophone notes into the office - she'd swapped the standard ringer so she could differentiate her phone from those of her colleagues.

She balanced the mugs and began to walk back but realised the second bar of poorly sampled notes hadn't been blown by her desktop performer. She got back to her desk and looked down at the missed calls on the screen. Private number. She shrugged, then left again, this time with no trumpets serenading her. She dropped her mugs in the kitchen and headed to the lifts, giving a few polite nods on her way, and deliberately slowed down by the uniformed officer to see who he was trying to impress. She was met by the empty brown eyes of Bonnie who worked in Cyber Security. In one hand, Bonnie held a small document, and in the other were several copies she'd just made. A small plea for help in those eyes was exchanged in that brief second. It clearly said she just wanted to get back to her desk, dump the copies then head home. However, Bonnie's politeness was probably enough to make her miss one of her regular trains back home. Kim gave a kind smile and a loud, "See ya," which was enough to break the conversation and give Bonnie an opportunity to slip away.

Kim looked over her shoulder while she waited on the lift, to see Bonnie walking back to her desk and the officer looking after her with his arm on the doorframe. He looked round to Kim just as the lift arrived. She returned her least sincere smile of the day and entered the lift. Kim put her rucksack on both shoulders now and paused to look in the lift mirror. Her black and grey hair was pulled to the top of her head in a bun, with more than a few strays having escaped. It now dangled past her brown eyes and floated freely below her jawline. She blew a couple away through the side of her mouth, and they floated up softly with her breath then came to relax in the exact same spots. She snuggled into thoughts of getting home and slipping into a bath. The universe had other plans for Kim, however. Once she stepped out of the metal sanctuary of the lift her phone began vibrating in her trouser pocket. She pulled it out and saw it was one of her reports, Bola Cassin. She answered.

'Bola?'

'Hi Kim. Sorry to disturb you,' said a voice carrying a light northern accent underpinned with a touch of French, a charming mix that she could listen to for hours. Bola worked with Kim in MIT. He had been with them for one year. He'd moved down from Manchester Met for a promotion into MIT. He was eager as a beaver, but still a little unsure of his place and the hierarchy down here. The stream of crime moved differently in Sussex, but it still flowed. He'd latched onto Kim after a friendly lunch, and subsequently, she'd become his unofficial mentor.

Officially, she was his boss, but she was very hands off. She had received a lot of calls from him regardless.

'Not a problem. Did you just call my desk?' She knew it was him of course. 'Yes, that was me. Have you left for the day? Sorry to catch you on the mobile like this but I... I've got a bit of an odd one. You free to chat?'

No, she didn't want to really. Could he phone back after her bath?

But it's an odd one, Kimi.

'Yeah, sure. What's up?'

6

Bola Cassin hadn't wanted to disturb Kim, but he was glad
she was on her way over to the scene of the crime at 33
Marsh Avenue. Secretly, that's what he had wanted. He
knew she relished people asking for her expertise and Bola
knew she would get stuck into this one. Curious was the
name indeed for the scene he was looking at. A quiet
street, a trendy renovation and a dead man who shouldn't
have been there - possible signs of a second person.
Whether it was an accomplice or murderer, was not yet
known.

There were no signs of forced entry, and some initial
on-site prodding suggested no signs of trauma to the
victim. Bola would say *victim* in his paperwork, but clearly
he shouldn't have been there, so *suspect* might end up
superseding that. It wasn't the oddest scene he'd ever
come across – people have their bizarre fetishes – but he
couldn't shake the uneasy feeling in his gut. The longer he
stayed in the living room, the more he felt he was missing

something, almost to the point it was making him a bit sick, as though he should run. It was an odd sort of nausea.

His thoughts wandered again to what it might be, then a broken sob came scuttling through the gap under the door. He'd been holding the owners of the house in the kitchen away from the scene while they composed themselves. He would start the questioning prior to Kim's arrival. He didn't like to look useless or unsure of his actions in front of Kim.

The family seemed truly shocked and unaware of the events that may have led to this man lying dead in their house. They said they'd been shopping then had dinner out. They could also show a dated and timed receipt. "There will be CCTV footage!" said the mother, hysterically, when Bola had arrived, trying to wipe her hands of whatever had happened here. Bola had learnt the hard way to not trust anyone at a crime scene, and also that playing by the book could get people in trouble. Instead, he had to adapt to situations and opportunities as they presented themselves.

Bola was new to murder investigation and he had to quell his constant curiosity of crime scenes and stay as professional as possible. Any crime scene created a volatile atmosphere. Emotions were high and people could flip at the drop of a hat. One of his first scenes in Manchester, where he'd taken a naive stance on an active domestic disturbance, had landed him in hospital. While shielding who he thought was the victim at a scene on a Salford estate, his kidney soon met the business end of a flathead screwdriver from behind.

Reports had come in from neighbours that the couple in question had been arguing and banging about their flat.

After a forced entry with his partner, the scene presented a scrawny man in his thirties trying to push his wife off him as she clawed for his throat. Given the fact he was less than half the size of his wife, Bola felt the need to protect the man.

As Bola held the man behind him, his arms wide, checking his partner was restraining the woman, he felt a punch in his left kidney. A punch that hung around a little too long – a warm punch. An intake of breath followed by a shooting pain where he'd never felt one before, convinced him he'd just been stabbed in the back. He collapsed to his knees in panic as he reached around to put some pressure on the wound. The man, who was later charged, fled the scene instantly, not wanting to hang around and fight the Manchester Met along with his scrappy wife. A small operation and a few weeks of recovery later, Bola considered everyone a suspect regardless of their size, what the scene said, or even if they carried a pulse. He still knew how to do things by the book, but the book itself was gathering dust on the top shelf.

He realised his right hand had found its way across his body to rub the spot the screwdriver had entered. He caught himself and thought it was time to head out of the room to talk to the family in the kitchen. He moved towards the door and surveyed the scene once more. It was very odd indeed. Bola tilted his head to get a different perspective on the suspect or victim.

It was a peculiar position to be in. The body wasn't sprawled or crumpled in a heap, which was often the case when someone had been knocked down. It was fairly well aligned, all limbs parallel to the torso, head perfectly straight, as if someone had delicately arranged him so. But, his face was frozen in discomfort. Bola thought on it a little longer then handed it off to his subconscious to mull over. On opening the door to the living room, he caught the end of a conversation coming from the family in the kitchen.

'...to worry about, darling. Mummy and Daddy will...'

The conversation ended sharply. Clearly, this family knew the secret sounds their house made when people were traipsing around it. Bola finished closing the door, walked the short length of the corridor and turned into the kitchen. He instantly felt the nausea settle.

Odd.

The house was a work of art. It was an old generator store expertly converted into a two bedroom residence. A deep parquet ran throughout the brick structure and was complemented by polished metals and reclaimed wood. Bola clocked several pieces of furniture in the hallway alone that probably cost more than his car. This was a rich family with an expensive house - attempted robbery was the most likely explanation here. The family, consisting of mother, father and daughter, sat at a glass kitchen table surrounded by gloss white kitchen cabinets bouncing the lights from above. Bola smiled warmly and moved towards the worktop opposite the family, then leaned against its white, grey-veined marble. The marble struggled to sap any cold from his body through his jacket, but it was hard against his lower back.

'Officer, do you have any news for us? I'd really like to know what's going on.'

It was the mother who had spoken first. White female, forties, blonde, blue eyes, slender build. She looked Bola directly in the eyes, her hands on the table, as if showing she had nothing to hide. The father had one arm around their daughter who had been crying. A few scrunched tissues lay on the table

'You and I both,' he replied.

'Was he murdered?'

Bola let that hang in the air and pulled out his pad which already had a few top line notes that the previous officer had shared with him on arrival. He refreshed his memory; Mr. Anthony and Mrs. Jeannine Howard, both architects, married sixteen years. Daughter of eleven, Ivy. Owners of this property for seven years, outright. Claim to have returned home around 19:15. Unlocked the front door, no signs of forced entry, dropped their shopping in the kitchen. The daughter then found the body in the living room when she went to watch TV. Shortly thereafter, 999 was called. Registered time of call 19:19. First officers on site 19:29. Family waiting outside the house. Paramedics on site 19:33. Body declared dead on arrival 19:35.

Bola looked up from his pad. The scene remained the same, but all eyes were on him now.

'I've been given a rundown of the events from my colleague. I'd just like to go over a few points if that's ok with you both?' The parents nodded silently. Bola continued. 'On returning to the house, did anything seem out of place from outside?'

They all exchanged nonchalant glances, shaking their heads in unison.

'No. Nothing that comes to mind.' This time, the father spoke up. White male, late forties, black hair, brown eyes, athletic build. He had a familiar Lancashire accent that Bola couldn't quite narrow down further. Bola had been in the U.K. for eight years now, six with the Manchester Met. He had dual heritage on account of his French father, but it had still been a painful process. He enjoyed pinning people to their hometowns and found the British dialects fascinating.

'Do you leave the windows open when you leave the house?'

'No. We're always very sure about shutting up, top and bottom,' Mr. Howard said. 'Most don't open due to the nature of the building. The narrow ones.'

'Front door locked on arrival?' Bola asked.

'Yes. I remember fiddling with keys.'

'No signs of forced entry?' he asked.

'No, no,' the father replied.

'I see you have a back and side entrance. Were they also locked?' Bola leaned away from the counter and looked out of their kitchen window to the garden.

'Well, we didn't check that at the time. But it's always locked,' Mr. Howard replied.

Bola turned back to the family and made a note on his pad. The first officers on site had found the padlock off the gate.

The Howards exchanged glances.

'On entering your house, was anything out of place inside?' Bola asked.

'No,' Mrs. Howard answered, assertively. She clearly wasn't satisfied with her husband's responses and didn't want any more notes to be made.

'No noise? Odd smells? Mess?'

'No, we keep a very clean house and I would have noticed if anything was out of place,' Mrs. Howard replied. The daughter shifted a little bit under her father's arm.

'And which room did you enter first?'

'We made our way in, shutting the front door behind us,' she said.

'And that's when you saw the body?'

'No. First, we went through to the kitchen to drop off the food as we normally do. We always shut the living room door when we leave.' Mrs. Howard looked embarrassed now, but continued. 'I always worry that someone will be able to see through the letterbox. We've got a very interesting house and people can get nosey. It was Ivy who found... that man.'

'Well, it seems you're very studious with your routine,' Bola said. This perked Mrs. Howard up again.

'Now, Ivy, is it?' Bola asked.

The little girl winced and looked up to meet Bola with her puffy bloodshot eyes. She leaned into her father a bit more.

'It's ok darling.' Mr. Howard's warm northern voice pulled his daughter in closer. 'I'd really prefer you direct questions to my wife and I, detective,' he said.

'I understand. Could you please explain what your daughter saw there, Mr. Howard?' Bola wouldn't push it, yet.

'Well. She must have seen that chap on the floor. We heard her scream. Piercing it was. I ran through and thought he was alive at first, so I pulled Ivy behind me. You would too if you saw a stranger in your house – and think he's alive, that is. A stranger is one thing, but dead? That's a lot going on. When I realised how still he was, lying there, it kinda looked like he was... like...'

'Uncomfortable,' Ivy spoke up. She seemed to scare herself with the sound of her own words.

'Ivy, darling.' Mrs. Howard reached across the spotless table to hold her arm.

'He did, Mummy.' Bola used this moment to softly nod her to go on. 'I was like excited to get into the front room to watch TV. Like really excited, actually. Anyway. I saw him as soon as I opened the door, then I like… then I kinda realised something was wrong. Like he shouldn't have been there and I screamed. It's a bit like a dream. Then Daddy came through…' her voice started to break off and eventually she buried her head in her father's chest and sobbed. 'I just wanted to go into the living room so bad.'

'Shhh, shhh, shhh. It's ok, my darling.' Mr. Howard's warm voice covered her like a blanket.

Mrs. Howard, heartbroken at her daughter's sobs turned to Bola.

'What are we going to do? We'll have to move into our summer property. We can't live here knowing, or indeed *not* knowing, what horrors happened in our living room. Poor Ivy will be scared to death of that room, of this whole house. I can barely stand it myself. I feel sick to my stomach.'

From the depths of her father's chest, Ivy said some words but Bola couldn't make them out. Mr. Howard patted her head. 'Shhh, darling.'

'But, daddy,'

'Ivy, that's enough. Quiet now,' he said.

At that moment, Bola heard a familiar engine outside. He walked across to the other window which looked out to the front. Kim was already on her way to the house, squeezing past vehicles.

Mrs. Howard went on. 'When will you be taking the body, detective?'

Bola turned to face the family one last time.

'We'll be a while yet. We need to identify him first. I'm sorry this has happened in your home. But give us some time and we'll find out what went on here. I'll get my colleague to come through and discuss the next steps. Are you familiar with the vehicles on your street?'

'As in, whose car is whose?' Mrs. Howard replied.

'To a degree, yes.' In such quiet roads, the residents tended to become familiar with the way the street looked. Hopefully, some curtains were twitching when the suspect broke in. 'That silver estate out front, for example.'

'I... I'm not sure which one you mean,' said Mrs. Howard. She looked to her husband for help but he simply shrugged.

Bola wrapped it up. The Howards looked unsatisfied. He nodded once more then called for the officer on duty and went through to see Kim.

7

Caz was halfway through a packet of crisps when she heard a sound at the door – two knocks which thumped off the solid wood. She took another crisp and placed it on her tongue, enjoying the popping sensation of sweet and sour in her mouth. She stared at the ceiling wondering who it might be. A door-to-door charity worker? Their friendly, yet overly familiar, neighbour? She bit down on her crisp, now enjoying the texture. She lazily asked their digital assistant the time as she took another crisp and laid it once again on her tongue.

'It's eight-forty p.m.,' replied a robotic female voice. It was a bit late for a charity worker. Adrian had said he'd be back around ten-ish after climbing. Plus, he had keys. Forgotten his keys maybe?

No, he took his car.

Another knock on the door. Four knocks this time, and firmer, louder.

'Ergh, not interested,' Caz said to herself, but the second bout of knocks did make it seem more important.

These are my nights.

Whenever Adrian said he was busy after work, Caz got a little excited at the prospect of some shitty TV and nibbles. As much as she loved him, she also loved some time alone. She heard mumbling at the door. It sounded like a couple of voices. Male and female.

'Mrs. Turner, are you home? It's Sussex Police,' said a calm female voice.

Caz's stomach immediately fell through her body. She sat upright from her reclined position.

Police? It's Adrian. He's dead.

She let the packet of crisps slide onto the sofa as she stood up and made her way to the door. She felt light-headed, as if most of her weight was still there making an indent on the sofa. She held out a hand to brush the wall and steady herself as she went. It was already trembling. On her way to the door, every step seemed to take her three. She reached their large wooden door and saw two figures through the frosted panes.

Caz exhaled, not realising she had been holding a breath in. The air was very thick all of a sudden. Her stomach felt like it was at the bottom of one of her legs and it was desperately trying to pull her heart down too. She snapped the latch and pulled the door open.

Please don't be dead.

Someone had stolen a car, someone was stabbed on the street, something to do with her sister, perhaps?

Would that be any better?

Caz shook her thoughts away and tried to think straight. She was letting her mind run amok.

She was met by the warm smiles of two plain-clothed officers: a tall man sharply dressed in a midnight suit, and a woman equally sharp in a grey suit. She had a little silver seagull brooch pinned to one of her lapels. Caz let her eyes rest on this.

'Mrs. Turner?' said the woman, 'I'm DCI Chowdry. This is DI Cassin. May we come in?'

'What's happened? Is it Adrian?'

'Might we be able to come in, Mrs. Turner?' she kept her tone level, not giving anything away.

'Please…' Caz's voice broke and her hands went up to her mouth. 'Please. Is it Adrian?'

'Mrs. Turner, may…'

'Is he—' Caz didn't think she'd ever had to say these words out loud, although she often had nightmares of it. She saw the truth in their reactions. Why wouldn't they have said no already?

'Is he dead?'

The words felt like tar as they left her mouth. She wished she could take them back, to pull out that nail she'd just sunk into the coffin. The officer gave a warm smile but said no more. Everything had gone deathly silent. A pressure immediately filled Caz's ears. This was a scene she'd never wished to find herself in, yet was deeply familiar for all those nightmares.

Caz immediately switched to red hot anger, an intensity she had never felt before. She wanted to reach out and rip that sweet, smiling fucking head off the officer. She was going to do it too. She took a powerful step forward but her feet didn't follow. Instead, her head was fast making its way towards the floor. She didn't know if she was flying or falling.

Caz heard the sound of an engine, an engine that was carrying her away. The next thing she knew, she was standing in a clinical corridor with people talking, but she wasn't taking the words in.

Next, she was in a small room behind a sheet of glass, and laid out in front of her was a metal table on wheels. Something was on top of the table covered in a crisp pastel blue sheet. The sheet was pulled back and she saw Adrian's sleeping face.

What's he doing here? Is he not uncomfortable and cold on that metal?

Someone asked if it was Adrian.

'Yes. Of course it is.'

Her hands felt hot. She looked down to see she was cradling a cup of tea.

Ooh, I like tea.

'Murdered?'

Who?

She stood outside her house, not sure what to do. Someone knocked on her own door for her.

Oh, that's nice of them.

Her door swung open and she was met with the sight of herself.

Oh no, that's Mona. That's Mona, my sister.

Mona started to cry and Caz thought she might cry too.

That felt like a good idea.

It had only just gone eleven-thirty p.m. when Caz stirred at the sound of keys jingling. She wasn't fully aware she had fallen asleep, and was dreaming, at that. She thought she'd never sleep again. Yet, it was the one thing she had longed

41

for more than Adrian when she began to get her sanity back. Something to escape the pain.

In her dream, she had been taking random items out of drawers and placing them into other drawers in a bright red room. The set of drawers were vast, yet she never had to move her feet to reach any of them. Some items were hers, such as an old wooden jewellery box her grandad had given her. It felt familiar as she had handled it, inspecting it for a moment and feeling the grain of the wood under her fingertips. Other items she'd never seen before – bits of scrap metal cold to the touch and some mismatched socks she would have never bought for herself.

Regardless of the item, she went through the same process. Opening the same drawer, removing the item it contained, inspecting it briefly, then filing it into another drawer that was already open and pushing it shut. It seemed there were always drawers open, ready to ingest what she was discarding, never diminishing in number. When she returned her gaze to the central drawer, it was always closed, as if giving birth to the next item in secret. Was this some Freudian metaphor for rearranging life? It was only when she took out Adrian's car keys, obsessively organised by size, coloured and numbered, she realised the sounds weren't in her head, they were coming from downstairs.

She lifted her head but heard nothing but breathing, lots of breathing. She held her breath and could still hear it. Again, she had to gather her thoughts, then remembered her sister was in bed with her. One big puddle of tears squeezed onto a double bed. Releasing her breath again she listened once more. Nothing. She let her head flop down onto the pillow. What was that feeling in her stomach? Had she been expecting Adrian to return after an impromptu night out on the town? He'd done that what, twice over the course of ten years? Could this really be a third time and this was all one big misunderstanding?

One big misunderstanding.

Yes, she liked that. One big misunderstanding, all the while managing to evade the police, break into a house and leave a lifelike, but dead, version of himself for someone to find? She let the pain wash over her as she let Adrian die once again.

The pain became increasingly satisfying each time she let it lap over her body. She could see them becoming friends for the foreseeable future, a thought that oddly satisfied some as yet unknown thirst.

She lifted her head sharply once more. That was definitely a sound from downstairs. Something *was* going bump in the night. Her mind once again flitted to Adrian and the image of his ghostly body bumping drunkenly into furniture downstairs, longing for his mortal wife. While enjoying the dark comedy of this, somebody close by whispered her name. She turned to see Mona outline. She had sat up in bed having also evidently heard the most recent noise from downstairs.

'What was that?' Mona said.

Caz realised her mouth was very dry and tacky with sleep, but the fear had just sucked the rest of the moisture out. She swallowed hard.

'There was something before as well.' She slowly swung her legs around and found the ground, while she instinctively reached to grab Adrian's stubby crowbar that he kept nestled by the bedside cabinet. A recent addition that he'd take out and inspect every night before bed, as if someone might have swapped it for a fake during the day. I wonder if this could have helped him tonight, she thought?

What was he doing in that house?

She felt for the bar between the gap and found its cold edge with one of her fingers. She shuffled it forward and grabbed it steady in her palm. The feeling was familiar to the metal she had handled in her dream moments ago. Perhaps her brain had already organised a plan of attack for whatever was about to happen. She began to shift her weight forward to rise, bar in hand, when she felt a tug on her shoulder. She jumped in her high state of alert.

'What are you doing?' Mona whispered.

'I'm just going to investigate,' Caz replied, more calmly than she felt.

Mona loosened her grip a little, then squeezed hard again as if that momentary lapse of concern might cost them both their lives. Sensing the internal fight in Mona's head, Caz tried to release her grip with words again.

'But what if it's—'

'It's not Adrian!' Mona half-shouted back, breaking the whispering threshold. This caused them both to shoot a look at the open door. Nothing stirred in the shadows.

Caz still couldn't believe he was dead. She had built haphazard narratives in her brain about Adrian's false demise. What paths he could have taken to evade all this business and miraculously come home. Some narratives only survived a moment until she found a hole in the plan, and crushed them like a house of cards. Others, she managed to get skyscrapers from, almost reaching the top floor. But each narrative, regardless of its structural integrity, was destroyed when the sight of Adrian's dead face - the very face she'd identified that evening - came swimming into view. It wasn't Adrian downstairs. He was dead. He had been murdered or…Well no one knew what he was doing in that house.

What was he doing in that fucking house?

Mona released her grip, spun off her side of the bed and began rummaging through her bag. Caz slowly stood as she watched. A floorboard creaked, but it wasn't from her weight. It had come from the hallway. She tried to shake the rest of the sleep from her brain to remember if anyone else had come to support her and stay over that evening.

Did you also forget your parents were dead, luv?

She only had Mona now.

The next moment, a smell reached her nose, a smell she knew well. Not the clinical smell of hospitals, not the dank smell of a rotting corpse, nor the smell of her own vomit coming up through her nose. She smelt Adrian. Not his cheap eau-de-toilette aftershave, which usually wore off by noon, but his sweet-smelling grassy musk. Caz turned towards the door to meet this musk, all the while her mind raced. Adrian was back.

I fucking knew it.

It had all been one big misunderstanding, or maybe even a dream. She didn't care. All she wanted was to hold him and end this nightmare. Just as the shadowy figure appeared, her subconscious argued all the narratives she'd made, pleading the case it couldn't be Adrian, that it was an intruder, or she was just hallucinating. Caz had tried to keep Adrian alive, but deep down she knew the hope was brittle. She had seen Adrian's lifeless face in person. The police had his car, phone and wallet.

The figure stepped forward very casually, as if it was in its own house. She needed to stop this intruder.

'Caz?' it said.

She had just got her wish. It was Adrian, intoxicating the air with his musk. But her body was already on the defensive. The bar was already flying. She didn't put her full weight into it. In fact, the rest of her body didn't move. Her right arm did all the work. It must have received a private and direct order from her subconscious without consultation of the heart. An order to take down the intruder in her house. Because this couldn't be *her* Adrian.

Her arm arced silently through the room. Caz's mind whirled. The only thought that filled her head after the impact was that human skulls were harder than she thought, judging by the amount of feedback she got through that solid metal bar as it made a connection. At least now, she knew it was real. She watched absently as the figure stumbled back, lost its footing and crashed to the floor. The house fell silent again.

8

Adrian was floating on his back. It felt like water, but thicker. Had he fallen into some custard, or was he still tripping? He tried to feel out the substance with his fingers but nothing came into contact with his senses or gave resistance to his fingers.

Whatever it is I need to clean it off - immediately.

His head felt very heavy and he felt it sink. The substance passed over his ears and the sound changed. It felt similar to the pressure of water. Panic reared. Was he going to drown in this stuff? What was he going to do when it covered his nose, his mouth? He tried to swallow and prepare himself, going for one last gulp of air. He opened his mouth but no air came, only the thick substance, slowly cascading inwards. It filled his mouth, its taste metallic. He tried to flick it away with his tongue but it felt as if someone had removed it. Where the hell was his tongue?

I'm going to die, I'm going to bloody die in this custard and all because I had a mushroom tea.

He began to lose track of where he was, coming in and out of his own thoughts.

Breathe you numpty. Forget about the trip, pull your bloody head up.

The substance slopped into his nose. *Now* he was drowning, his last periscope of hope blocked with the still unknown substance. With what felt like the world turning on its axis, Adrian flicked his head upwards, away from his custardy doom. His whole body moved with him until he felt his bum hit something hard, his feet following shortly afterwards. He came to his senses just in time to hack up whatever was sliding down into his lungs and spit it from his mouth. He gasped for air, it came freely, but at the cost of fiery needles exploding in his lungs.

Adrian found himself slumped on a hard chair. The last of the substance, which turned out to be blood, dripped between his knees in one long saliva-esque stream. His body gave a quick shiver and greeted him with a throbbing headache. *What fresh hell is this?*

He let his head hang a little longer over his knees. He was almost doubled over in this chair but something held him in place, preventing him from toppling. His other nerve endings told him he was tied to the chair. The headache was growing. It appeared he only had clear vision in his right eye. The left was very blurry. He brought his feet into better focus and saw he was wearing the same trainers he'd worn earlier - whenever earlier was. He took a deep breath and hoped his brain would take over on the breathing front from now on. The legs of the chair hugged his calves on either side. It seemed they too were restrained. He examined the legs of the chair whilst he let his head hang heavy.

That looks familiar.

It was an Ercol leg – he'd recognise that shape anywhere. Many a weekend had been spent finding second hand deals on antique furniture. He had some Ercol chairs. In fact, this was *his* Ercol chair. He knew this because it sat on a very familiar patterned carpet that lay upstairs in his spare bedroom. His mind started to fire up and immediately began obsessing over the endless tasks in his head, of which restoring these chairs was one of.

Glue the loose joints, sand the chairs, prime the wood.

He raised his head as much as he could and let his good eye spin around in its socket to take in the lower third of the room. He was in his own house. Adrian began to relax a little but was still very confused. How had he got here?

No. Sand the chairs first, glue the loose joints, prime the wood.

Maybe this wasn't to do with the mushrooom tea he'd had.

'Flying, frisbee... foxes,' he said to himself. He had no idea what that chain of thought was.

Sand, glue, prime.

'We have to keep his head up. He might have choked to death,' said a female voice. It startled him but he finally registered the owner.

Sand the chairs, glue the joints, prime the wood.

'Caz?' He tried to turn his head in the direction of the voice. He got it a little higher this time, and saw what was unmistakably his wife's figure a little to the right, but he couldn't quite see her face. His head gave an almighty thump and he lowered it again.

'Argh. Caz, what is going on? I'm tied up here,'

Still nothing.

'I'm bleeding.'

Teeth feel fuzzy. Need to brush them.

He heard footsteps from the other side of the room. He turned his head as much as the pain would allow but his dud eye didn't register anything and his nose got in the way of his right's view.

'Who are you?' the new voice said firmly. It was less familiar but he knew it.

why can't I think straight?

It spoke again. 'Who are you? What are you doing here? And what have you done with Ad—'

'Stop!' Caz said. 'Don't say his name. Don't give away anything.'

The footsteps retreated a little.

'Answer us. Who are you?' said the unknown voice again.

'Caz, who is this? That is *you* right? I can't see. My eye...' With a great heave Adrian pulled his head all the way up setting off fireworks in his mind. It was Caz, for sure. But what the hell was going on? She looked terrified. The fireworks crescendoed and Adrian began to lose a little grip of reality again. A wave of nausea ran through him.

Wasn't I sick earlier on, he thought?

Yes, the mushrooms.

No, it wasn't the drugs…It was something else.

That seemed very clear to him all of a sudden although everything else seemed foggy. He began to fall back into the bloody custard and braced his body for the impact.

9

Mona rushed forward to catch this Adrian lookalike but it was too late, he'd somehow managed to flop over his restraints and the chair had gone skidding out under him. Caz hadn't budged an inch. She was still in shock. What had they expected? They weren't a couple of gangsters who did this for a living. Caz shot a frightened look at Mona and it made her crumble inside. Her poor sister was confused, torn between love and fear, mourning her husband, then in walks this doppelganger. Mona couldn't deny they were identical, other than the fact this one was still breathing, for now.

But how could it be?

She was just as confused.

'Mona,' Caz's broken voice carried across the quiet room. 'Mona, help me. I don't know what to do. If you weren't here, I'd be sure I was going crazy. This *is* Adrian.' Caz stepped closer to the man's side and stood, her hands fidgeting at her mouth, lost. Mona ran over the events of the last few hours again to try and make sense of this scene.

One simple answer was that this actually was Adrian, and both the police and Caz had identified the wrong man. The other, more outlandish answer - the answer which wasn't really an answer at all but a vast canyon of questions - was that this man and the man the police had found were both Adrian.

As much as her analytical self wanted the first answer to be true, there was a hum of curiosity vibrating inside her. A flood of paranormal possibilities wove over each other, gagging for her attention. She squished this down quietly and got back to the matter of her dear sister being torn between two futures that were both uncertain right now; she was either a widow or she was not.

'Caz, let's step out for a moment.' Caz didn't move.

'It'll just be a moment. I want to check something with you, away from... him,' Mona said.

'But, his head? Shouldn't we stay with him? I'm worried he's seriously hurt, that I seriously hurt him, I did that Mona.'

Mona had just finished an advanced first aid and minor trauma course at school, so the knowledge was fresh in her mind. She knew he likely needed a once over at the hospital - as well as a going over from the police.

'Caz, we need to phone 999.'

'No!' Caz snapped, staying put.

'Why not? He needs help - you hit him with a crowbar!'

'Because. Because, what if someone is after him?'

'After him?' Mona asked.

'The police said it could have been murder.'

52

'But Caz, even if that were true whoever did it thinks they managed it. They fled. Besides, we don't know what he was doing in that house.'

'What are you getting at?'

'I…' Mona started.

What am I getting at?

'You think he was having an affair, don't you?' Caz said.

'What! Caz, no. I don't…I haven't got a clue what's going on. Can we please just talk away from him. I'm just trying to look at this objectively.'

'Maybe he was having an affair…' Caz said to herself.

'No, stop. Look. If that man *really* is Adrian, we need to tell the police he's not dead. They got it wrong. You got it wrong.' Caz looked at Mona confused.

'Mona. If we do that, the killer might come back to finish the job,' Caz said. Clearly the time for reasoning had passed.

Mona would have loved to phone the police. They needed an authoritative figure to put the two men side by side, declare the whole thing a mix up, and tell Caz to stop walloping her spouse with a crowbar. It was clear that Caz wanted to keep him here. Mona tried to extract her sister from the man's presence once more.

'Caz, we can leave the door open. Let's just move away a little bit.'

Caz returned her gaze to the man one more time. She took a deep breath and knelt down next to him. She hovered her hand near him then made her way to the door, looking back so often she might have well have walked out backwards. Mona followed, eyeing the ties around the man's wrists and calves as she went. He wasn't going

53

anywhere fast. Caz positioned herself with a good view into the room. Mona stood to the side and allowed Caz her vista.

'I think you should call the police,' Mona said.

'Mona–'

'Not to report this. I think you should ask to see Adrian again. The Adrian at the morgue.'

Mona could see her sister's mind processing these words. She was running a little slower than her usual self at that moment.

'You're in shock, sis. You were hardly yourself when you came back. You were all over the place and you said it was a blur. A second look would be good, if that's allowed?'

Caz had always been the hardiest sister, always the first to pick herself back up again, and get straight to helping others off their bums. Most of the time, she didn't even fall over, she just tripped a little. Mona tried to recall whether Caz had always been like this, or if it had been part of her transitioning to the head of the family after their parent's passing.

'You know, I can barely remember standing in that room,' Caz said. 'I think I just nodded at the officer maybe.' Mona watched Caz move into second gear.

'It was seconds they had that cloth off him. There was glare against the glass, it was so bright, and I think my legs wanted to get out of there as soon as possible. I wasn't even in the same room as him for fuck sake. That could have been, anyone. Christ. How shitty is that? You lose your husband and they make you see him through some shitty glass six feet away?'

'Ok, good. This is starting to feel like some kind of

plan now. Because we can't keep that man tied up forever. We're not very good at it.' Mona allowed herself a chuckle.

'Well, that might not be any man. That might be Adrian in there, Mona. He even *smells* the same. I wonder if...' Caz had whipped back through to the room before Mona could go on. She snapped on the light, dropped to her knees and prodded him

'Adrian,' she said firmly. 'Adrian, it's me.' Mona watched as Caz now cupped the man's face and tried to level it off with hers for a good look. 'Adrian, what did we eat the first time I ever stayed over in London? What did you cook for me?'

Mona silently entered the room and stood next to the crowbar. If that wasn't her sister's husband she would drive her car right into the school building and scalp Priya with a strimmer. His familiar face rooted under the dark tangle of hair – now slightly blood-clotted hair. The police had identified the wrong man. She hoped she had done a good enough job on that gash. Caz gave his head a little shake that made Mona wince a little.

Be careful Caz!

'Adrian, what did you cook for me?'

'Caz?' he said. The man's voice was equally familiar, yet slow, which worried Mona some more. 'What, what are you doing? Get this light off. God that's bright.'

'The first time I stayed over, when we...you know. What did you cook for me?'

'What?' He started to fight with his restraints more and growl like a grumpy dog. Caz let his head drop, softly this time, and stood back a little.

Perhaps it wasn't Adrian after all. The imposter had

failed whatever test Caz had given him. He soon stopped struggling.

'Darling, please,' Caz said, 'What did you cook?'

Mona thought he had passed out again. She was getting increasingly worried, and walked forward to inspect him, but was stopped in her tracks by some grumbled words.

'Didn't cook.' A long rattling breath. 'Pizza.'

Caz spun around to Mona, tears already spilling out of her eyes.

'It's him. It's him, Mona.'

10

Teddy spent his first night in a parallel universe as lonely as a proton in a hydrogen atom. He lay curled up on the icy white sheets of the bed like a seal hiding from circling orcas. His body didn't shiver at the thought. If something could end the sorrow he was in, he would gladly take it.

Dead.

Murdered! Another part of him said.

He closed his puffy eyes and breathed in a rattling breath. The air struggled to fill his lungs and images of Adrian once again bounced around his mind.

Teddy had spent half the night mourning the loss of Adrian, and the other half trying to figure out what had happened. He did have one hypothesis: that it was *his* fault. He pushed it aside for what felt like the hundredth time and waited for it to come ricocheting off the walls of his skull and torment him again shortly. He needed to get up. He had a whole new world to explore and here he was, skipping like an old record.

A whole world, to explore alone.

That didn't take long: hello darkness my old friend.

Teddy had so much more he wanted to teach Adrian, his insatiable thirst for knowledge sustained them both. From the first question he'd asked in Teddy's class, Teddy knew he was special - in many ways. Never had a masters student looked at problems the way Adrian had, even as a mature student. He was so unrestrained in his thinking. It was a gift. He'd never loved anyone so intensely as Adrian and the reciprocation was mutual - and Teddy wasn't easy to love.

Teddy was obsessive, unconventional, blunt and distracted. When he'd first invited Adrian over to his house - if you could call it that - at 33 Marsh Avenue, he thought he'd blown it. Being a live-in guardian of an old generator building, he hardly took care of the place. There was evidence of habitation, but objectively you'd struggle to guess which of Earth's mammals had taken up residence. From the crumbling mortar, lack of amenities and laboratory-come-bedroom, Adrian stayed completely silent on the private tour. It was only on viewing Teddy's collection of old TVs that Adrian finally burst out laughing at the state of the place and broke the ice. They then made love for the first time there on the floor. Their inaugural lovebed had become Adrian's deathbed. Teddy sobbed once more on the cold sheets. He stared down the chandelier for sometime afterwards wondering if it would take his weight.

Get a grip, man. Work needs to be done.

With great effort he kissed the image of Adrian goodbye for now, and sat up in the bed.

The late winter sun was seeping around the edges of the shutters on the tall Georgian windows. The sun had always been a friend to Teddy, the warmth of the distant star both invigorated and calmed him. The silk sheets helped his weary bones slide off the bed as he made his way to the window. Teddy pulled the shutters open. The sunlight hit the middle of his chest and fanned outwards as he opened them their full width. He felt the light push away the darkness that had started in his heart. He instantly felt better the moment he was completely bathed in its warm glow. The heat had been building through the panes and it was perhaps the first time that year he had felt the actual warmth of the sun on his skin, not just its light.

Teddy wasn't sure if it showed on his face, but he smiled. He stepped up to the window and looked out to sea. He knew this part of town well, yet he'd never viewed it from this angle. Raised up on the side of the small cliff where the hotel sat, the view was unobstructed, unlike at sea level. The morning was clear. He could just see the start of the Kent coast to the east, the sun sitting low and lonely in the sky, and the Isle of Wight standing proud to the west. No man is an island, he thought of his isolation.

I'm certainly not the Isle of Wight.

'It's all so similar,' Teddy said to himself. 'So similar, yet…' He looked down at his hands, turning them over as if they were also foreign. His mind was still scribbling away at possible equations to answer what had gone wrong, and although that frustrated him, what frustrated him more was the fact it tarnished their achievement. Teddy may have been the only one who made it, but it had been *their* achievement nonetheless. He looked back out to sea and tried to focus on the achievement, for if he didn't, Adrian's death would be in vain.

'I travelled across to another universe. A parallel

universe.' He said the words out loud to help him ruminate, the same thing he did when working on scientific problems. Repeating them over and over until something clicked and they made sense. It was a habit formed in childhood. If someone heard a child say such words, they might think it adorable, creative. If someone heard an adult say them out loud, they might think them a little odd, mad. Teddy wondered how many people would even understand what he said if they heard it. It was always Adrian's child-like mind that had helped them to strive forward, naive to the negativity that plagued a scientist's mind.

'I travelled across bloody universes,' he said, more confidently to himself, his chest puffed and his shoulders open, 'and I'll bloody do it again.' Teddy recalled the sensation he'd felt on the night of travel: it was extraordinary. There was nothing on Earth like it. He wanted it. He *needed* it. Everything had fallen away in that moment, the universe had *invited* him to cross. But why?

Because it felt bloody good, that's why.

He needed another hit. He looked back down at his hands and saw they were trembling. They were eager to explore, to feel, to touch this world - the spoils of his journey. He reached out and pressed a hand to the window. It was cold, despite the sun. He let a shiver run up his arm and envelop his whole body, relishing in the feeling. He thought it felt out of this world, *whatever* world you came from. He stepped back from the window and eyed the wall. He ran his hand along the surface, the coarse limestone lightly grazed his palm. He could feel every peak, every trough, as though it was scratching an itch he didn't know he had.

He spun around and headed into the bathroom, allowing his hand to skim over the top of the bed sheets as he went, the smooth silk greeting him like an old friend. Stepping into the bathroom, he began to strip down, throwing his pyjamas to the floor. Teddy stepped into the shower, cranked the temperature dial all the way to cold, until it went no more, then opened the tap looking straight up into the shower head. A little creaking of pipes and a couple of gurgles later ice cold water hit his face like hailstones, he gasped and spun around to let it hit his back, writhing in the sensation. He felt alive. He had been through a terrible ordeal but he was alive, more alive than he had ever felt.

'I fucking did it!' He spat into the shower.

Teddy left the heartbreak hotel and headed out to a local jewellers. Bank accounts were too abstract to rely on in a parallel world. Money, you could hold - and they had taken a large amount - but there could have been complications with currency. But gold, silver and precious gems were a safer bet. The fact Teddy had these trinkets reassured him he could keep things moving while he figured out what to do next. He was no longer able to get a loan from his parallel self, wherever this world's version of himself may be.

The jewellers was nothing special. Faded black paint, gold lettering and freshly cleaned windows – all the better to see the jewellery with. He raised his eyes to the signage. "Ottoman's Opals", it announced in fine gold serifed font. Teddy stepped in.

'Hello,' Teddy said over the chime of the bell.

'Hello, sir.'

The saleswoman was beaming away. He took her lead for now, she'd soon find out he was here to sell, but he knew it would work out well for both of them by the time he left.

'Crumbs, it's cold out there today.' He let out a light giggle and she joined in. They both relaxed a little. 'I pass through a fair bit and have been meaning to bring a few items by. I see you also buy?' Her smile faded a little.

'Yes sir, that's a service we can help with. Please, take a seat over here.' She led Teddy to one of the glass counters and pointed to a mahogany chair donned with plush velvet padding. Teddy smiled and sat down. At that moment, a man walked onto the sales floor from the back room, giving Teddy a warm smile. He fiddled with something in a cabinet then returned to the back room. Teddy was sure that was just a "no funny business, mate" performance. No bother, nothing funny about selling jewellery.

'So, what do you have, sir?' The woman took a seat on the other side of the counter and let the twinkling of the stones encased in rings below shimmer off her face as she smiled.

'Well, I've a few family items. I'm certainly not getting any use out of them. Let me get them out for you.'

Teddy leaned down to unzip the bag, it was Adrian's detachable rucksack. As the zip opened, a musk started to fill the air – deep but sweet. Adrian's musk. Completely unprepared for this, Teddy felt a pang in his stomach, and the memory of Adrian shot up though the figurative dirt he'd buried him under that morning to get out of the hotel.

Ever the pragmatist, his subconscious quickly ran in with a shovel and began heaping more dirt on top of the bubbling emotions. He would need a digger soon enough.

Teddy composed himself and pulled out the necklaces that were wrapped in Adrian's clothes. He placed three golden crucifixes, their chains all tangled together, onto the table. He went back into the bag, this time holding his breath as he went down.

'May I?' the woman said, gesturing towards the necklaces. Teddy looked up.

'Yes, by all means.'

She untangled the chains expertly and inspected them, one by one. Teddy's next hoard contained an assortment of rings. Gold and silver bands with a mix of coloured stones and diamonds. The woman raised an eyebrow. With each new reveal she sat back more in her chair, and eventually looked round to the door that led off the sales floor. Everything on the table was Teddy's. He had plenty more to go, but that was all Adrian's.

No use now you killed him.

'Stop it!' he said out loud.

'I'm sorry?' she replied. He zipped up the bag and sat upright in his chair with a smile.

'Apologies. Just telling myself to stop being… sentimental.' He smiled but judging by the woman's reaction he'd done a poor job of it.

'Well, that's everything. Wow. I haven't laid them all out before. Quite the haul, isn't it? Just bananas left in there now,' he motioned to the bag, 'unless you also buy exotic fruit for cash?' Teddy really tried to pump up the nice guy act now. He reckoned there was close to six thousand pounds worth of goods on the table. He already knew he would take just over half that if needed. The woman let out a soft laugh and widened her eyes. 'Indeed. Quite the mix you have. Family items, you say?' She inspected the rings one by one.

'They are.'

'And you're looking to sell it *all,* are you?'

'If possible. But I'm in no real need. I just thought I'd bring it all down at once for ease of appraisal. I've really no idea about the price of these things. Is it weight, carat, age?' Teddy played the fool just enough to keep her interest piqued without seeming desperate.

'Lovely. Well, in the interest of not wasting your time, please bear with me a moment while I grab the manager.' She popped her chair back, apparently waiting to be released.

'Oh, of course, by all means.' Teddy continued to smile, thoughts of Adrian knocking on his mind's door.

She made her way to the back. Teddy leaned back into the chair and crossed his legs, then looked around the room marvelling at its similarity to the Ottoman store in his world. It wasn't similar - it was identical. But why should this store be the same, and yet other aspects of Furlong differed? On the way here, he'd passed a petrol station he regularly used in *his* world that was a pub in *this* world. Teddy began to hypothesise that because each world was inhabited with billions of lives, the odds of each and every person following the same path were immensely unlikely.

Fascinating.

The order of the room started to unsettle him. Everything had a place. Where was the entropy? How could anything be achieved if one fussed over the inevitable: all will succumb to chaos one day. Before long, the woman returned. She hadn't brought the man he'd seen earlier, but another woman. Adrian realised this woman was also the manager of Ottoman's Opals in his world. This was the first encounter he'd had with a parallel version of someone. It took him off guard. His mind began to excitedly bubble. The jewellery seemed unimportant - insignificant.

'Good afternoon sir, my name is Maggie. I own and manage the store here. Ttwarna here tells me you wish to appraise a few items?' Her eyes rested on the myriad of mismatched jewellery on the desk, calculating away.

'Well,' Teddy tried not to study her too much, 'if possible, yes. I'm not quite sure how this works. I was saying to Ttwarna here that most of this has just been sitting at home. Some from my late father, those would be the crucifixes, then some from my Christening, but mostly from my grandparents and extended family.' Maggie inspected the items more closely. Teddy took this chance to inspect her more thoroughly; same haircut, a severe bob; same suit, pastel pink; married, platinum glistening on her finger. She suddenly looked up and caught Teddy staring. He rattled off some lines but his mind wanted to ask Maggie a thousand questions.

'My parents were the only ones in their families to have a child, and just me at that, so I tended to inherit most of the family heirlooms.' He gave a little chuckle after this spiel. It wasn't all lies. He also hated leaning on his Catholic heritage but that had always been the plan.

'You're looking to sell it all?'

'Yes, that's right. What kind of price will I be looking

at?' He wanted to speed this up now, he couldn't focus any longer.

'Well, we'd need to appraise each item individually, but in the thousands I expect. However, I'm not sure we could take it all. It's also a case of what we could look to resell here in store and the current market values.'

Teddy ignored all that and focused on the money. 'Well, a few thousand would certainly be ok with me. Are we looking at around three?' He could see the manager having a moral struggle here. He had undercut the real value by a stupid amount, more than enough to move things along at pace. She quickly made her decision.

'That's a very good estimation sir, considering you were unsure of the value. I'll just give these a quick once over and we'll ensure it's in line with current rates. We wouldn't want to leave you short.' A friendly smile crept onto her face, but Teddy imagined she desperately wanted to lick her lips.

Teddy shut the door to the jewellers twenty minutes later with a straight four thousand in his breast pocket. She had begun to take the piss a little and he fought to get the price up on principle. Besides, things hadn't gone to plan so far; he needed to be thrifty. She was still getting a tremendous deal. Adrian's contributors to their hoard still slept in the bag. The dirt rumbled inside him again and his legs started to carry him back to the hotel. Back to the abyss.

11

Kim crushed the remainder of her cigarette on the wall as Mrs. Turner drove into the mortuary carpark. They had offered to send a vehicle but she was insistent she didn't want to cause any bother, and the drive would do her good. It was only a ten minute drive after all. It was a ten minute drive to everywhere in Furlong. It took ten minutes to get from east to west. From the South Downs to the beach, ten minutes. Even if you tried to take a shortcut from one side of the train crossings to the other, it was still ten minutes. Those things would always catch you. This town didn't like anyone to cheat it. Furlong dictated the pace of life, Kim thought as she poked the cigarette butt into the wall bin.

Mrs. Turner had yet to get out of her vehicle by the time Kim had crossed the car park, Kim slowed her pace then eventually stopped a few parking spaces away. She didn't want to rush her. It wasn't unusual for spouses to want a second look. The first encounter is always a shock if it's to confirm an identity, and such a tremendously hard task for the individual. Most barely remember it. A second look does tend to be more emotional, more definite, more loving, but it can help with the long and winding road of mourning. The only oddity here was that it had only been a day. They'd allow this visit, but Kim wasn't suddenly about to open a museum for the dead. The coroner still had to perform the post-mortem to determine the cause of death, work needed doing. The longer this dragged out the harder it would be for Mrs. Tuner.

Poor cow, Kim thought as the cold bit her face in the exposed car park, away from the safety of the smoking shelter. Mr. Hoarding's death was still shrouded in mystery and that tended to go hand in hand with the grieving. The more mysterious the death, the harder it was for loved ones to let go.

Forensics had worked into the night, sweeping 33 Marsh Avenue down, but there was little to tell that they didn't already know. Someone else had likely been there, but the lab was still looking at this. However, the lack of trauma to Mr. Hoarding's body didn't make the other party a killer, but Kim knew that person was key to Bola unravelling this one. Kim was merely acting as a Family Liaison here while Bola led the case. Or so she told herself. It was a curious case for sure and she knew she'd stick her oar in.

The one point of entry, unforced, seemed to be via the side gate. From a purely observational point of view it looked like Mr. Hoarding had waltzed into the side of the house unimpeded through the open doors, laid down for a sleep and died. The other party either came with Mr. Hoarding or may have come in afterwards looking for their own place to die and saw that 33 Marsh Avenue had already been taken. Kim liked to keep things light in order to cope with the misery of life in the Murder Investigation Team.

Mrs. Turner finally got out of her vehicle and made her way towards the entrance.

'Mrs. Turner,' Kim said, while rolling onto her tiptoes in that very polite British way. Caz looked round then after a brief moment of recognition, she stopped and smiled. 'Oh, hello…' She'd forgotten Kim's name, of course.

'DCI Chowdry. But, as I said yesterday, please call me Kim.'

'Well then, you better call me Caz,' she replied, happily.

She's positively beaming.

An alarm bell chimed in Kim's head. Who on earth was this happy woman in front of her? Mrs. Turner seemed like she was going to visit a friend in hospital who had just had a baby, not her dead husband. All that was missing was a card and a bunch of flowers.

'Shall we?' Kim offered towards the mortuary building.

Caz nodded and they walked in step towards the hospital. Kim put it down to shock for now - humans were funny creatures.

'Will your sister be staying with you a while?' Kim asked.

'Oh, yes. I think so. Our parents have both passed.'

Caz left that sentence hovering in the air but Kim thought it best left alone. This woman had just lost her husband, she didn't need to drag skeletons onto the pile. They walked in silence up the mortuary steps. Kim found silence the best course of action in these circumstances and didn't attempt to ask how Caz was feeling. Open questions were not a good idea.

The electric doors shuddered to life as they approached. Once through the second set, Kim was met by a familiar medicinal musk, the same that would be found in a hospital. This building was long past its use-by date. The building was actually part of the old hospital that stood there before. Faded turquoise floors speckled with shimmering fragments greeted them as they entered the corridor. Kim was a regular face here – business not pleasure – and nodded to the receptionists as she passed.

Kim continued to lead them to the mortuary through winding corridors and closed down sections of old hospital built over the years, each a time capsule to that period. The turquoise floor gave way to gleaming tiled surfaces, harsh concrete, unkempt parquet and even a questionable beige carpet so worn and compressed from the workings of the hospital it could have been wood. The sound of their footsteps changed in timbre with each new terrain, bouncing off walls that still housed local and inoffensive art intended to calm those walking by, or perhaps spark some joy during a difficult time. They approached a set of double doors and Kim pressed a buzzer.

Through the chicken wire glass, Kim saw a young male porter approach who she hadn't seen before. Slicked black hair revealed pointed features and a solemn face – a face for the job. An electrical click came from the door as the electromagnets disengaged and the face reappeared through the crack.

'DCI Chowdry?' His voice was slow and drawn out.

God, what a cliché.

Kim returned a smile. He held the door open and

allowed them to pass. Memories from cases past welcomed Kim as she entered. Each of the four rooms held echoes of despair that Kim would no doubt bring to her grave. This was where little Arthur had been reunited with his parents. His parents had silently clung to each other as their tears flowed. Protocol dictated that police presence was required in viewing rooms at all times, and that was the only time Kim had broken it. When parents were going through hell, so could the rules.

'Room three please,' he said.

Kim directed them to room three, then came to a stop at the door and addressed Caz.

'Are you ready Mrs. Turner?' Using her first name seemed too informal in this situation.

'Yes.' Her cheeriness *had* faded. The reality of her visit was setting in, Kim thought.

'We won't be viewing through glass today. Are you comfortable with this, Mrs. Turner?' She saw her resolve falter slightly but then a confident nod followed.

'Would you like a minute?' Kim asked.

'No. Let's go through.'

Kim pushed the door open and led them into a square room with one set of double doors on the far wall. The fluorescent lights buzzed loudly overhead. A few moments later, the far doors swung open as a stainless steel gurney was wheeled in with the unmistakable figure of a human draped in cloth upon it. The feet pitched the cloth like a sail, an invisible breeze softly blowing the bed forward into the room. Kim was hoping to see the coroner, Dr. Baker, bring in Adrian's body, but it was the solemn porter again. Kim knew Dr. Baker was overworked. Much like an owner of a budget hotel that had more jobs than staff. At least the guests didn't want for much. He brought the bed to a rest, stood straight and looked to Kim for instruction. Kim put her hand on Caz's shoulder and felt she was tense. Caz slowly looked round and nodded yes to the silent question. Kim returned this nod to the porter, an unspoken chain of command back and forth that would likely bring with it sounds of despair.

The porter pulled the cloth back to reveal Adrian's face then stepped away. The buzzing of the lights was very apparent now. Kim looked round to check on Caz. She seemed confused, almost as if she was expecting to find someone else under that cloth.

Poor cow.

She tilted her head to the side to get another point of view but the confusion stayed on her face. Caz took a couple of steps forward and Kim got the impression she'd forgotten where she was, but allowed her closer.

'Adrian?' Caz said to her deceased husband. This caught Kim off guard and her heart gave a little pang in sympathy. Caz took another step forward and the porter looked up helplessly to Kim for instruction.

Why hadn't Dr. Baker brought Adrian through?

Kim closed the distance in case she needed to take some action while moving around Caz to get another read of her face. She now looked as lost and defeated as she had last night, but it was still marred with confusion, as if she was trying to do some long division on the fly. She's just trying to comprehend this, Kim thought. But Kim's alarm bell rang again. Something was amiss.

'I don't understand?' Caz said, tears filling her eyes now. She moved very close to the body. Kim reached out and placed a hand softly on her shoulder for both comfort and restraint. There was technically nothing wrong with touching the body but it wasn't the 'done' thing, and no good could come of it. Caz took a step back and turned to face Kim.

'That's my husband. It's Adrian,' she said. Kim nodded back silently. They'd had time to check the correct records now and Kim knew this was unequivocally Adrian Hoarding, but they had needed Caz's confirmation the other night. Historically, Kim would associate this behaviour with the grieving process, coming to terms with the fact that this was indeed the body of a loved one. Some victim's families had even said to Kim over the years that they still expected to bump into the person they lost on the street. But there was something up with Caz she couldn't quite put her finger on. There was an intonation of real confusion, separate to the grieving.

'Would you like to step out a moment Mrs. Turner?' Kim asked.

'It's Caz,' she snapped back. Kim removed her hand and took a step back. Emotions were high. 'This is my husband.' Caz pointed towards the gurney.

'Caz,' Kim was sure to use her name now, 'this is a very difficult time for you.'

'Yeah, I'm aware of that. Thank you.' She had gotten prickly fast.

'Perhaps it's best we step out for a moment?' Kim nodded to the porter who stood frozen in time. Clearly this was not what he had signed up for, thinking he would get to poke around dead bodies alone all day. Kim had to widen her eyes for him to get the message and he finally covered up the body once more. Caz pounced, whipping off the sheet completely and clasped a hand on the body's

73

shoulder. Kim saw the flesh give way to the hand in its dead state, the muscles no longer full of life. Then came a scream. Kim took Caz's wrist and pried it off Mr. Hoarding's shoulder. At that moment, the double doors sprung open and Dr. Baker made her way swiftly into the room, surveying the scene as she went.

'Michael, Jesus. Don't just stand there boy.' The porter jolted back to life and gathered the cloth off the floor and clumsily threw it back over the body.

He mumbled some words in apology.

'Don't mind with that, just please wheel out Mr. Hoarding.'

'No. Nooo,' Caz screamed. Dr. Baker took up residence by Caz's other side and gently placed her hand on her other arm in a manner only a trained doctor could achieve. Kim tried to match her grip. She didn't know if it was Dr. Baker's touch or the retreating of her dead husband on the gurney, but Caz instantly began to settle down, and by the time the porter had wheeled the gurney out of sight, Caz had given up her fight. Kim released her grip, as did Dr. Baker. She ran her hands through her hair.

'This just doesn't make any sense!' Caz said. Kim had never seen an expression quite like it. Confusion streaked her brow while her mouth twitched in a grimace of anger, but it was her eyes that were the most bizarre. Kim had heard the old adage that they were a window to the soul, and in this she felt they deceived Caz a little. Kim had seen those eyes a hundred times in her line of work. It was part of her job to read people and she thought she was pretty darn good at it. Those eyes held a secret. Caz turned on her heel and left the room. Kim let her go, her trainers squeaking on the tiles as she went.

12

'He doesn't just look like you, Adrian. He *is* you.' Caz's words came through muffled against Adrian's damp shoulder as they lay on their bed together. Adrian was still sore, but he let Caz nestle in. Caz and Mona had done a good job of tying him up. Adrian felt a twang of pride knowing that, should he suddenly die, Caz could more than take care of herself. She had always been a fighter, more so than him.

'I know you Adrian – the greys in your beard, the way your right nostril is bigger, the pores in your nose, your whole body. I thought I was going crazy in there, I *must* have looked crazy. I whipped the sheet off him and everything. It's like Madam Tussauds got their hands on real flesh – your flesh.' She pulled away and met Adrian's eyes. Those beautiful blue eyes. Not big and whimsical, but truly perfect and beautiful. A blue to wash away others' blues, encompassed by a delicate event horizon of black. There was no escape once they sucked you in. They were sparkling with a sheath of tears but he sensed they were born of relief more than anything.

It felt good to hold Caz again, properly. Coming home to the blunt end of a crowbar hadn't taken a toll on their relationship, but the confusion that followed had left Adrian swimming in a thick dark sea around a very slippery island. Just as he climbed ashore and got a grip, something gave way and he'd be plunged back into the dark depths where his mind raced away beyond the normal bounds of its obsessions and compulsions. Her touch gave him comfort, security, and grounded his sea legs. His head still throbbed worryingly, but his vision had returned to both eyes. Under any other circumstances he really should get down the hospital.

'I can't explain why, but it *is* you. He's Adrian too.'

Caz hadn't been hit with a crowbar. If she thought it was Adrian in the mortuary, then it was him. He didn't know what powers were at work here but his body shuddered with fear and mystery. They both thought someone was out to kill him. He pushed the panic away, placed a kiss on Caz's head and left his lips there. He held her close as he tried to lighten the mood.

'Look, before we get into this, can we stop calling that thing "me". It's creeping me out. Can we just call it... Dave?'

Caz chuckled and nodded in agreement then ran her hands up his back to his head.

'Dead Dave?' she suggested.

'I love it.'

'Are you ok?' Caz asked.

'Yeah. The thumping is quieting down,' he lied. 'I'll survive.'

'Not your head. With all of this. You're technically dead.'

'Huh?' He hadn't really thought about it that way. He'd been more concerned that someone might be after him. He thought about the implications. 'I guess I'll have to be.' He tried to bring his attention back but saw that Caz's side table was all out of order - he normally did this for her every morning - but he was a little behind. He started to arrange the pieces in his mind before he made his move.

'Well, when shall we ring the police?' she said.

Get rid of those mugs first. Push the clock to the edge. Then –

'What? No!' he replied.

'But, why not? They can help straighten this out. You can't just *be* dead,' said Caz, peremptorily. Adrian wasn't sure if it was the headache, but announcing himself to the police sounded like madness.

'Because clearly someone has tried to, well successfully actually, murder me.'

'But, the police can protect you, Adrian.'

'Well, they didn't protect me the first time,' he said, rather annoyed, and now trying to point a finger at a guilty party. Caz was right, he wasn't ok with this. Someone had killed him and he was taking it personally. Adrian tried to tweak the scenario to imagine one where a friend or family member had been murdered. He would be beside himself, full of grief wondering how and why it could have happened and why the omniscient police hadn't been there to stop the murderer.

'They didn't know someone was after you,' she said.

'But now *I* do, and that gives me the upper hand.' Caz pushed him away.

'Upper hand? Adrian, this isn't some fucking film. This is serious, you can't play dead. You could be in real danger if someone really is after you.'

'Which is why we need to keep this to ourselves.' Why wasn't Caz getting this?

'What the fuck are you on about?' she shouted.

'Keep your voice down,' Adrian said, his eyes shot to the open window. They weren't secluded, they were end-of-terrace. At that moment, the bedroom door swung open and Mona jumped in without a word, the crowbar, which had now got a taste for blood, raised up, ready to strike. Her eyes darted from Caz to Adrian but she looked confused. He saw the bar falter slightly and then she regained her grip as if Adrian had sensed this weakness. Before he could say anything, Caz burst out laughing. It was a hearty cackle. She placed one hand on her stomach and one on her mouth in an attempt to stifle it. It was no good, it took over and Adrian felt the air quivering as it filled his ears, and soon enough he was also chuckling. Mona looked nothing more than confused. Her eyes continued to dart between the two of them.

'What? What's going on? I heard shouting,' Mona said.

Adrian tried to catch his breath and Caz was now hunched over the edge of the bed. She tried to speak through her gasping breaths while waving a hand at Mona in some attempt to communicate the situation. Through tear-filled eyes, Adrian saw Mona lower the crowbar.

'What's going on?' she chuckled. 'Is everything ok? I thought...'

'You look ridiculous,' Caz managed to blurt out.

'Hey. Well, I thought something had happened.'

Adrian had now lost it and buried his head in the

pillow. He'd forgotten about the fresh bandage near his temple and pain soared again. He managed a childish "oww" and the laughing continued. His little plight set Mona off too as she brought her hand up to cover her mouth. She quickly raised the bar again and hissed,

'Hereeeeee's Mona.'

The three of them were in hysterics for several minutes letting the stress of the day evaporate away. The questions could wait.

13

The next day, Adrian was still bedbound. Caz placed Adrian's tea on the bedside table. She caught him playing with the bandage on the side of his head and wasn't sure if he was doing it on purpose to make her feel bad. Either way, she did feel guilty, hence the tea. Adrian was normally the one who brought her hot drinks in bed. She joined him and cupped her mug of coffee. She breathed in the warm nutty aromas and started to wake up a little more.

'The police have been in touch after my little outburst,' she said.

'Oh? What did they say?'

'They've asked if I would like a DNA test to confirm the identity. Clearly, they think I'm going crazy.'

'I think they'd be going crazy if they knew the truth. This is great though right? Now we can be certain?'

'Yup.' She felt like no one else really believed the other body was identical to Adrian's. She would give the police everything they requested; toothbrushes, dirty pants - the lot - for her own sanity more than anything else.

'So…' she said softly, 'do you need to tell me something, then?'

Adrian turned to Caz confused. Bless him, she thought. I'll just wind him up a little.

'About where you were?'

'Ah,'

'Yes, *ah*. A drug dealer, Adrian. What are you, fourteen?'

'Hang about. It's not because I want to go get high with my friends and roll around in the daisies.'

'Your OCD?' Caz said. Adrian receded into himself, picking up his tea to occupy him.

'Yes, my OCD.' He blew softly onto his tea. 'I know you hate it. I hate it too, Caz. I don't like living with it one bit. The doctor didn't help, did it? I don't know what else to do. It's getting worse.'

'Go to therapy.'

'I've tried that.'

'Adrian. You went once.'

'Yeah and I hated it. They just sat there. How is that meant to help me?'

'I don't know how many times we've gone over this - you get what you give.'

'Oh like you would know.'

'Don't you fucking dare,' Caz fumed. She knew he was alluding to the fact she'd never seen a therapist after her parents had died. That was different. Caz didn't *need* therapy. She just got on with it and moved forward.

Adrian and Caz had met after her parent's deaths and they had managed a happy relationship just fine. It was his

OCD that was the problem. She squished a squirming part of her that wanted to speak and moved on as she always did. Adrian blew on his tea. The man was terrible with heat. He loved hot drinks, but for the most part, by the time Caz thought her coffee was too cold to drink, Adrian would think it was just right. Caz took a sip of her coffee, it lightly grilled her taste buds.

'So,' she said, her anger already gone. 'What did you get up to while you were in Cable's Wood? You were gone for hours. Imagine if you were here when the police called? That would have confused the hell out of them.'

'Well, maybe that would have been easier?' he said.

They both thought about this briefly as they tended to their drinks. Last night, after more prodding, and almost begging Adrian to go to the police, Caz finally saw things from his perspective. Someone had killed *an* Adrian, regardless of motive, and it wasn't worth the risk of exposing the real Adrian. Not quite yet anyway. They weren't in a film, but it sure felt like they were. After checking with Mona, who had become their new sounding board of reason, they had all agreed to let this play out for just a day or two more. Adrian went on with his story.

'Well, none of it really went to plan. I've never been into a drug den before, so it was all uncharted waters anyway.'

'Drug den? On Marsh Avenue?'

'Ok, I'm embellishing. It was a lovely place. He was really nice actually, considering.'

'Considering the drug dealing, or…'

'Well, yes. Considering I'm pretty sure what I did was bad etiquette, in *anyone's* house.'

'Stop dragging it out, what really happened?'

'I was sick all over his front room.'

'What?'

'Yeah. And kind of on his slippers a little.'

'He wore slippers? L.O.L!'

'He did.'

'I thought you said you *felt* sick last night. Not that you were sick.'

'Well, I was in a bad way yesterday and couldn't really be bothered to take you through it. I just needed to sleep.'

'Christ. What an entrance.'

'Should have turned away at the door. My belly started to rumble just then.'

'Oh. So it wasn't the drugs?' she asked.

'You know. I thought I knew what it was yesterday, like I'd put my finger on it.'

'As in, a bad sandwich or something?'

'Err, yeah. Kinda. I'm pretty sure something else started it. Although I'm sure the mushrooms got things going a little faster. Not uncommon apparently.'

'Oh yeah?' Caz said, playing along. 'Connoisseur now are we?'

'Well, I've got to sample the merchandise. He had three different types.'

'Oh, how fancy. So, what did they do when you threw up?' Caz asked, curious as to how it played out for her husband. 'Was it just Michael, the dealer and you?'

'Yeah. They were lovely. Michael was a bit embarrassed I think. But the drug dealer was lovely – Andy. He must have been pushing eighty, little old hippy dude.'

'No!' Caz said in astonishment. She conjured up images of an old, free-loving hippy cleaning up Adrian's vomit while throwing a peace sign to say it was, "all groovy man".

'Yeah, yeah. That's why I agreed to go. I wouldn't have just gone into some random dealer's house that I'd heard someone talk about on the street.'

'Well that's good to know, darling,' Caz quipped, patting his leg.

'He showed us some family photos after I'd settled.'

'Aww.'

'Haha, I know. Said he probably should have let me try something a little less potent as it was my first time. I helped him clean up once I'd come to. Thank God he had laminate flooring. Michael just…'

'Wait. Come to?'

'Caz, I was gone. I completely blacked out. They said they were on the verge of calling 999.'

'Oh my God.'

'That's why I don't think it was the mushrooms and something I'd caught. They both agreed they don't work like that. It was so odd. It felt like I was on some kind of rollercoaster, my head and legs being pulled in different directions. It's all a bit fuzzy, but when I came to, I honestly felt fine, if a little happy.'

She went to scold him then remembered she'd just experienced what it was like to have your husband seriously hurt, like dead hurt. She counted her lucky stars and let Adrian go on.

'Anyway, after that I was on guard for another vomit, but I felt better. It had completely passed. That's when I told him I hadn't been feeling well and he said he believed me, but he was clearly just being polite.'

'And did this happen when tried some?' Caz asked.

'I promise I'm not being secretive, but I can't remember the order. I recall being very hot. I threw up over and over. My skin was prickling like hell, like it was trying to rip itself away from me. My insides were on fire, my soul was on fire.'

'Oh.' Caz recoiled a bit at that turn of phrase. Why had Adrian used soul? It made her shiver.

'Then, I passed out. I was still covered in sweat when I woke up and my abs were a little sore. But I felt fine.' Caz looked at Adrian, puzzled.

'How odd.'

'I know, right? Fucking weird. Bless Andy, though. He didn't try to throw me out in case I went again. We just chilled and talked about other things.'

'Like what?' Caz asked. Adrian shrugged his shoulders at this.

'Not much. Just chatted.' Caz never got this about men. How did they manage to spend hours talking or messaging on their group chats all day yet know nothing about what was happening in each other's lives? It bamboozled her every time.

'I can't believe this was all at a dealer's house.'

'Honestly, such a nice guy.'

'So, what happened with the car then?' Caz asked.

'It's such a mess and the more I think about it, the more it creeps me out. So, I said sorry, thank you and goodbye. I didn't tell them but I was too scared to drive and was going to get in my car then phone for a taxi. Then, as I went back up the road I saw a lot of people standing in the street, which instantly made me paranoid. Then I saw the blue lights and the police tape, my car was stuck inside the crime scene! So then I started to panic even more and the last thing I wanted was the police to question me about why my car was there and what I'd been up to. So I quickly turned around and walked off, but my phone and wallet were in the car. All I had were my keys. Took me nearly two hours to walk back from Cable's Wood – it's bloody far on foot. I was too paranoid about my car and the severity of whatever crime had happened that I tried to stay off the main roads. If it was really bad, which I kind of guessed, I imagined the police would figure out it was my car and come calling. And, low and behold. They did!'

'Yes. They did.' Caz felt her tear ducts quiver. She went to speak but couldn't get anything out.

'I know, I know. I'm so sorry darling,' Adrian said.

'Not my favourite time that,' she managed, a bit more comfortably. 'Well, you should be sorry, but really we should be more concerned about the fact there's another you in this world, dead and laying in a fridge somewhere.'

'And there's another thing,' Adrian said.

'I know.' Caz knew what he was going to say but didn't have the mental capacity to try and tackle that too.

'It's all a bit too perfect of a coincidence isn't it? Dead Dave happened to die in a house that my car happened to be parked outside of.'

'Adrian, I can't.'

'I know…'

'Let's try and focus on positives - do you at least think the mushroom's worked?'

'Ha. Well, I feel a little more disorganised than usual. And it didn't take me two hours to get to bed last night. If you can refrain from smacking me tonight we'll see how long I take.'

'Maybe I cured you.'

'I hope you have.'

Caz watched through hazy eyes as Adrian took a sip of his tea, no doubt now cool enough for his delicate tongue. She smiled and brushed his cheek with the back of her fingers, glad that *her* Adrian was alive and well. She continued to watch him then burst into tears realising what she had nearly lost and miraculously got back. Caz never wanted to feel that darkness again.

14

Kim saw Bola sitting at his desk as she stepped out of the lift. She looked down at the forensic report she had just been handed downstairs. He'll love this, she thought, feeling the weight of it in her hands. Sorry trees, looks like this criminal didn't care how many pages he'd rack up. Bola had his headphones on which allowed Kim to get right behind him and toss the report over his shoulder so it landed slap-bang on his keyboard. This apparently didn't faze Bola. Instead, he gently pushed it aside, held the delete key to erase the gobbledygook of letters that now lay on his screen, removed his headphones and turned to face Kim.

'That's a big report,' he said.

'So, you already know what that means, don't you?'

'I was right?' He smiled.

'I never said you were wrong.'

'But you didn't agree with me.'

'Ok, but the bigger picture goes beyond you being right, Bola.'

'Oh I know. But it gives the picture a nice frame to sit in doesn't it?' Although she thought it impossible Bola managed to squeeze a bit more distance out of that smile.

'You were right.' Kim pulled round her chair and took a seat. 'The positioning of Adrian. He was dragged into that position.'

'Yes!' Bola slapped his knee. 'Someone *was* trying to remove the evidence.'

'Someone, yes. Or–'

'I only said there was someone else. I didn't say it was Mrs. Turner,' he said.

They both sat in silence. Kim knew Bola was uncomfortable with the idea that Mrs. Turner could be involved. Kim hadn't been able to shake the feeling that she was hiding something - in fact the feeling had been growing.

'Anyway. Whoever it was, it's not an easy piece of evidence to shift,' she said. Bola nodded at this.

'And what about Mr. Hoarding? Wounds, internals, what was it?' he asked.

Kim shook her head at this. Every department was still stumped on this part. 'Nothing to hang onto. Could easily be an undiagnosed health condition that went pop at the wrong time.'

Bola started to flick through the report.

'The DNA is conclusive,' he said.

'Yes. I'll give her a call to let her know.' Kim responded.

'Thanks.'

'What else does it say?' Bola asked.

'It's your hands. What am I, an audiobook? You may

have been right, but you're still going to have to do some more work, detective.'

Bola scoffed at this, obviously knowing full well Kim would have already told him anything worth actioning straight away. In truth, Kim had only skimmed through, the evidence of a second person being present was the main point, but she hadn't looked at the further bookmarks the lab had inserted.

'Give me the abridged version then,' Bola asked, putting the report down.

Kim took her packed lunch out of her bag. Her belly gave a little rumble at the sight of it. Clearly, that banana and coffee at six a.m. had run its course already.

'Oh you want the *abridged* version? Yeah, that's just on the front there and it says, *stop being a lazy git.*'

'Ok, boss.' Bola got the message and picked it back up while Kim finished unpacking her bag.

'Looks like he had a dodgy ankle,' Bola said after a time. 'Severe ligament damage it says here'

'Fascinating,' Kim replied. 'Twisted it on the way down to the shops did he?'

'Okay. How about this? Traces of hydrochloric acid high up in his oesophagus, throat and mouth,' he read.

'Foreign?'

'Unlikely.'

'So, he was sick?' she asked.

'Inconclusive, but likely. You wouldn't poison anyone with hydrochloric acid, the quantities would be too much. Maybe he was just struggling to keep something down? Maybe that's what got him.'

Bola leaned back again and stroked his stubble in thought, then nibbled his index finger for good measure.

Kim let Bola nibble away. This was his case and she wouldn't be holding his hand. She was off duty when she attended the scene, and in honesty, she only went to Marsh Avenue out of curiosity - she liked the fancy houses up there. However, as tempting as it was, she had several other cases to oversee in MIT. She'd be a sounding board, and slap him on the back once he figured it out. He was a good detective.

'So, two suspects,' Bola said over his desk.

'Or, one suspect and one victim, depending how you look at it.' She was busy but she still had time to wind him up.

'Please. Mr. Hoarding had no grounds to be there.'

'Maybe he was giving it a once over before putting an offer in?' Kim thought she'd test Bola's research so far. He scoffed again.

'Yes, Mum. I've done a ring around. They reached out to estate agents as soon as we told them we were done there. I actually need you to sign off so they can start viewings.'

'Didn't want to deal with the ghosts then? That's gonna get a lot of attention, house like that.' Kim asked, not at all surprised that Bola had found this out alone.

'Yup. Don't blame them either. A lot of people die in houses. Sure that could be enough to make you move. But potentially murdered, in these circumstances. That's some bad juju to live with, I think I even felt it when I was there. Almost nauseating.'

Kim caved in and popped open her lunch-box, removing a couple of leftover roasties from the night before. She convinced herself they were basically hash browns. She pondered Bola's last word: nauseating. Why did that resonate with her? She had felt something similar at Marsh Avenue. She thought back to unpick what it was but stopped herself. This was exactly what she was trying to avoid, doing detective work in her head for another case. She was just tired that night, that's all.

'Shame. Nice house,' Kim said.

'That it is. Nice area too. Plenty to poach.'

'Is that where your head's at then, attempted robbery?'

'No, not really,' Bola replied, almost as if he didn't want an explanation so boring and simple. 'I'm kind of floating around some form of infidelity.'

Kim couldn't help herself; she grabbed another roastie and scooched around the desk.

'Go on,' she said.

'Mr. Hoarding isn't a criminal. His history, data trail and character comfortably affirm that. Financially secure, mortgage regularly paid, plus overpayments. Doesn't need to risk anything for the small haul a family house would get him. But infidelity at a secret rendezvous–'

'Trespassing?' Kim interjected, dumbfounded that anyone would go to that length for a kick.

'It's exciting,' Bola said. 'Although I've no idea how they managed to break in, alarm and all that. Must have been a good thief if he was one.'

'Must be a bloody good shag.'

'What if it wasn't just a shag though? How about love?'

Kim choked on the dry potatoes and reached back to grab her water bottle. She washed down the lumps and took a breath, then resumed eating. Potato in one hand, water in the other. It was glorious.

'Ha, here!' Bola folded over the pages of the report and

placed it between their desks. 'Foreign DNA on Mr. Hoarding's forehead. Saliva.'

'No? A kiss?' She leaned over the document and read the lines Bola had his finger on. There it was.

'Bet you wish you had read it all now,' he said.

'Don't need to, looks like you're being *my* audiobook now. So, do you agree it could be Mrs. Turner?'

'You won't let up will you? Are you forgetting she has an alibi?' he said.

'I'm choosing to ignore it for now.'

'Alright. It could be. But I still think it's infidelity. Unless you plan on getting a warrant for *her* DNA?'

'Unlikely. Well, I hope we're both wrong,'

'Oh?'

'Bola. Look at me. I'm pushing fifty and I don't have a partner. If this is what it takes to get a kick these days I don't have it in me.'

15

Adrian was making dinner. He had all his ingredients laid out but he couldn't find the cheese grater. It was making him sweaty. It wasn't where it normally was, in the drawer next to the fridge. He started to blame Caz in his head – she never put things where they're meant to go. He'd have to do a dance now. Didn't she know everything had its place?

But why would she, this wasn't their kitchen after all.

The lucid half of his brain pondered this while the rest of him slithered through the dream.

He looked out the window to a plush garden. The tones were overwhelming, the grass was saturated to a burning point and the blotches of colour from the flowers stung his eyes so much he felt his head ache. He turned away and began opening the other cupboards. Large plates, medium plates, small plates. He opened some drawers to find boxes and boxes of cook's matches, but no cheese grater. What was he making again? Where was the cutlery? Maybe they could use the matches as chopsticks? All he knew was that he needed that bloody cheese grater. His fingers felt heavy with dirt, he'd need to wash them before continuing.

He closed the drawer and moved to the sink. He decided to try the cupboards again on the way. He opened the first, then someone called his name. It was a male voice he hadn't heard in a long time, and he couldn't quite place it by sound alone. He turned and was greeted by the smiling face of an old friend from school. His unkempt hair hung over his ears and forehead just as it had all those years ago. He had a smirk on his face like he'd just told a good joke.

What's he doing here? Crumbs, what's his name again?

'Thank you for cooking dinner, Adrian,' he said.

'Not at all. It's the least we can do. Especially after your help with the tests. I've never been good at English, have I?' Adrian's need for the cheese grater was increasing with every second and now he had to try and remember this boy's name or he'd sound rude. He always hated it when people dropped his name into a sentence and he couldn't reply in kind. He knew it was a test.

Oh God, what if he doesn't like my dinner?

'Would you like to come and play football? We're all going out now to the garden.'

Adrian thought this odd. Football? But dinner was nearly ready. Hadn't this boy grown up at all? How could he go round playing football before dinner?

He must not be doing as well as I am these days.

'I need to cook dinner. Need the cheese grater,' Adrian said with some frustration.

'Ok,' he said, undeterred. 'Quickly then, before it burns.' Then he walked off.

'Fine. Go play then, I don't need any friends.' Adrian spun back to the kitchen in search of the cheese grater again but there was no need. The stainless steel box was sitting on the worktop glistening in the sunlight. Plates of food had also appeared and the worktop was full of them.

'Shit, dinner's ready! Right, there's two, four, six–'

No wait.

'Three, six, nine…Ah, I've never been good at maths.'

He left the counting and went for the cheese grater but fumbled it.

Wow, that's heavy.

He tried again but stubbed his fingers on the top. Adrian's anger boiled, he needed to finish this dinner. With all his concentration, he grasped the grater with his outstretched palm and lifted it from the worktop. The weight remained but once it had cleared the worktop it became easier. Perhaps it was magnetic, he thought. Nick would know.

Nick!

That was his fucking name. He shouted it out loud.

'Nick!'

Adrian brought the grater up to his face. He smiled. He had the fucking grater and he remembered the boy's name.

'Nick, Nick, Nick,' he chanted. He leaned over the bowls of food ready to grate. He had made pasta.

'Nick, Nick, Nick,' he chanted again, this time a chorus of Nicks came wafting in through the open window. He must have scored a goal in the garden.

Go on Nick!

He turned to the window and saw familiar faces grinning and thrusting their fists in the air as they chanted along. Nick was playing with a whole team of Adrians.

'Nick, Nick, Nick,' they sang in his own voice. Adrian grinned back menacingly, he felt like his smile was ear to ear as he turned back to the bowls of food. He brought the immense grater up to his left temple and felt the cool emanating off the metal. He listened to the chants – constant, persistent, a steady 4/4 beat. He waited for the next bar to start, he brought his head back on three and held it on four. When they returned to one, he snapped his head forward, skimming it perfectly against the side of the grater. Chunks of stringy flesh flew off in flat noodle like waves and cascaded down to the plates. Some made their way into the bowl, others flopped over the side and spilled onto the worktop. He had to get his head back for the next beat. He brought his head back until he could see the ceiling and thrust it forward just in time.

'Nick!'

More flesh came off, but this time red. They looked like stings of beetroot. Back again, ceiling, forward.

'Nick!'

My God, this felt good.

'Nick!'

Yes, more. All over the dinner. Make it tasty.

'Nick!'

What if he ran out of head to grate? Should he leave some for the next dinner?

'Nick!'

Nah. Use it all.

'Nick! Nick! Nick! Nick!'

The chanting was euphoric, it filled his soul.

'Nick! Nick! Nick! Nick! Adrian!'

What the… They've changed the beat?

'Adrian. Adrian.'

What are they doing? That's too many syllables. They're ruining my dinner. He closed his eyes to focus on the new beat.

'Adrian?'

He missed the cheese grater completely on the next turn. He'd lost the beat. His whole arm was going numb and the immense weight of the cheese grater had returned. He felt his forehead connect with something hard and unforgiving. That didn't feel euphoric, it plain hurt. He opened his eyes to see what he'd hit. He thought it must have been the kitchen cabinet. He was met with the bedroom wall, dimly lit from a warm light source behind him.

'Adrian, wake up, wake up!'

'Caz?'

'Adrian?' He heard some relief in her voice. 'You're dreaming, you plum. Having a nightmare.' He turned to see her face and she gasped.

'What? What?' he said, shuffling his feet against the slippery sheets to pull himself up to sitting. Christ, his head was thumping.

'Your head. You're bleeding. It's all over you. Your cut, it's…'

Adrian reached up to touch his head but he didn't need to. His hand was already covered in blood dotted with lumps of scab. He'd been scratching his cut in his sleep like a dog after an operation.

'Ah. Fuck sake. Well, if it wasn't going to scar, it definitely will now,' he said.

16

Mona sat quietly in her car fiddling with her keys. She'd been there for nearly thirty minutes, parked in the multi-storey car park opposite Furlong Police Station. She kept telling herself she was doing the right thing. Yet, every time she looked out across the street to the top of the Police building she began to shake. The hurt voice of her sister flew around the car like a caged bird, "How could you do this to me? To us? They're sending me to jail Mona, are you happy now? You're such a goody two shoes!" it squawked at her.

Caz was smart, yet she'd never seen her sister behave like such a fool. How on earth could there be two Adrians? It just wasn't possible. Her sister was clearly still struck with grief and couldn't see the wood through the trees – she was seeing things. Objectively, it was absolute madness. Mona was the one who felt like she had her head on straight in this clandestine operation. Once it was brought to police's attention that Adrian was alive and well, they could all lift this veil they were living under, put Adrian next to the dead guy and clearly see they'd made a horrible mix-up. The longer they left it the worse it would get.

Mona shook again and had to close her eyes and take some deep breaths. She tried to relax further by listening to her surroundings. Outside, cars were whizzing up and down the multi-storey in search of spaces. There was an occasional toot of a horn signalling someone had blindly pulled out, and snatches of music or loud conversation could be heard as the cars passed behind her. It wasn't peaceful, but it was distracting. Mona imagined what madness might be going on in those lives at the moment and how minor they likely were by comparison. Someone late for an appointment, pretty minor; perhaps someone rushing into town to purchase a forgotten birthday or anniversary present, also minor. But really, they were just nuances on people in a rush. All these fake scenarios were just nuances of time, just people in transit in varying degrees of rush.

She needed to get this done, for everyone. She took a few more breaths with her eyes closed and tried to calm the rest of her nerves. This was it.

Just another couple of breaths.

Ok, this is it.

One more.

Ok. One more deep breath, really deep.

Yup, ok here we go then.

Before she could fool herself any longer, a rap of knuckles on her window made her scream and drop her keys into the footwell. She looked around in panic and met the piercing stare of an angry female traffic warden. She said something to Mona who was surprised she couldn't hear, even though the warden's breath had steamed up the glass. Mona went to click the window down but the car had gone to sleep. She went to fish her keys from the footwell, but her shakes had returned and her fingers danced around the footwell like the cast of Riverdance. She grabbed the keys and found the ignition with a little less trouble and clicked the window down.

'Yes, Officer?' Mona said.

Officer?

Clearly the stress had got to her and the warden's costume was a little too police-like. The warden seemed to like this form of address, and smugness washed over her face. Mona didn't think it softened her features.

'You can't sleep in here madam,' she said.

'Sleep?'

'Yes, sleep. I see there's no ticket on your car and control said you've been here for over half an hour now. I'm going to have to write you a ticket.'

'No!' Mona said.

'No?' the warden said back, clearly having heard it all before but nonetheless curious at how this one would go. If a warden could be this stern, how would the police react to Mona outing Adrian and Caz? Mona didn't want to get them in trouble, she was just trying to help.

'Madam?'

'Yes all right,' Mona snapped back, annoyed at the interruption of her thoughts. 'I'm just leaving. I'll go and buy a ticket for the hour.'

'I'm afraid that's not how this works,' the warden replied.

'You can't seriously be giving me a ticket, I haven't even left my car.'

'That's exactly the problem.' Mona didn't like the schooling tone of the warden one bit. She was the one who schooled.

'Well, unfortunately, I've a little trouble building myself up for these things.' The warden's face retreated slightly but she kept her ground. Mona pushed on. 'In fact, I don't think I'll even be able to make it into town now that you've upset me.'

'Right.'

'I'm happy to purchase a ticket, Officer.' She went for more brownie points. 'I'll even pay for two hours, but I think it's rather unfair that I be penalised for the time I take to compose myself. Don't you agree?'

'So, you weren't sleeping?'

'No. It's the middle of the day.'

The warden put her hands on her hips and surveyed Mona a little longer then came to a decision. 'Ok. Two pounds forty.' She held her palm out. Mona was about to question that surely she should go put the money into the machine but thought it best to play along and dodge the much larger fine. Perhaps the warden would pocket it, perhaps she wouldn't. Mona went into the ashtray and pulled out the change – thankfully she actually had some – and dropped it into the warden's hand.

'Thank you,' the warden said, like a school bully taking lunch money. Mona started up her car. The warden took up the space as she reversed out and bounced the change in her hand feeling its weight. Mona drove back down the multi-storey and pulled out to the street, opening all the windows to let the fresh air in and push out that fading notion: *the longer they left it the worse it would get.*

Someone would have to blow the whistle on this soon. Form some plan to break it to the police. For now, Mona's plan was to phone up her friends and arrange an evening out to forget all about it.

17

Teddy knew he couldn't stay in this hotel pining for Adrian much longer. His funds were limited and it was a very expensive way to mourn. Since the trip to the jewellers he hadn't left his room. He could downgrade for a time, but he'd likely just end up crying himself to sleep on cheaper sheets. What he really needed was a base of operations. He needed his home, his laboratory, *his* 33 Marsh Avenue. He had no idea if he'd even be able to get back through the bridge yet, let alone where he'd end up. Was the bridge still being powered from his world, making connections to this one as they dropped in and out of phase with each other? If it wasn't he'd need power. Did this version of his property still have the old generator in the cellar, or had they converted it into a hipster wine store or some other useless piece of shit?

'Fuck.'

He could try and run the bridge off the consumer unit with a few adjustments - maybe they still had the three-phase in there?

'Four hundred volts might do it.'

Might it?

He pulled the sheets tightly around him and sighed.

'I need Adrian.'

Teddy had undergone an immense change in character since Adrian had walked into his life just over a year ago. Prior to, his relationship with reality had been on a steady decline. Peers laughed him off with his attempts to consolidate and transcend parallel universe theories into practicality. Their incessant denial and inert minds infuriated Teddy, every fucking word had fueled his work. No one got it. As time went on Teddy eventually ended up working in secret - but even Teddy had to admit he had struggled to transcend the theory. He had become disorganised and chaotic in his work. Equations formed easily in his mind but he struggled to put them down on paper, they would flutter away as quickly as they came. Had anyone witnessed one of his later fits of passion they would indeed think he had gone mad. He had been called manic depressive in the past, but that wasn't true. He had either laughed those fools off or just receded into his work further - depending on his mood.

Teddy had always been convinced that parallel universes had existed - if you believed in infinity, there was no reason not to. The universe was constantly expanding: anything was possible. He smiled at the thought. That was exactly the kind of beautiful thinking that Adrian brought into his life. Anything was possible if you looked at it the right way. That's what Adrian had done, albeit accidently. His mind was free from all the knowledge that bogged Teddy down. He'd shown Teddy that the edge of the universe, something that was technically billions of lightyears away, also lingered unassumingly all around them - in the static noise of an analogue television signal. The cosmic microwave background. After Teddy magnified a few crucial areas with his own intelligence, it became so beautifully simple. If the edge of the universe was present, then all one had to do was step over it. *That* was the doorway to other worlds.

'Such a beautiful mind.'

But now Adrian was gone.

Teddy felt his mind slipping without his anchor, he was starting to revert back to his old unproductive ways. He was struggling to keep the theory straight in his head, even though it wasn't a theory anymore. Adrian had brought order. He had added the perfect amount of protons to Teddy's atom, stabilising his runaway electrons. Teddy looked up at the chandelier which hung in the room again. Would it take his weight?

Probably.

'Probably.'

If such things were to be done he'd still have to leave the room for... supplies.

Six hours later Teddy pushed against the revolving doors of the local library with his shoulder. The worn bearings creaked inside their housing then fresh sea air whipped Teddy's thinning hair off his forehead. He had got his mobile working again but was glad that, for whatever reason, his internet and reception weren't working in this world. A day in the library to think without distractions had answered a lot of questions, and it all seemed so clear now.

With hindsight, Teddy didn't feel stupid. This wasn't some GCSE level physics he'd miscalculated, it was interdimensional travel. Hell, it might as well be time travel. Teddy allowed himself a moment to wonder what was harder – time travel, or jumping to a parallel universe? He then had to remember that he *had* jumped universes. Now, he did feel silly. He tutted and shook his head gleefully.

'Silly, Teddy.'

Most of the time, it was hard to remember that this wasn't his world, his Earth, his Furlong. It wasn't as if he wore a bright wristband to remind him of the fact, or to differentiate him from those *born and bred* in this universe. What would it say? *Interdimensional traveller, Gold Band, VIP, Access all Areas.* Everything was so nearly identical. It was the people, or lack thereof, as he now hypothesised, that caused the differences. Humans shaped the world. Number 33 Marsh Avenue was not a disused generator store under guardianship in this world, but the key still turned the barrel in that padlock, and in his world that padlock had come with the property!

He heard blood pumping through his left ear as his mind went whirling off at speed. Teddy thought of this regular occurrence as his internal cooling system, like a computer's fan. When the workload went up, and his "central processing unit" sucked more energy from whatever reserves he had, his body tried to keep everything working smoothly by increasing the blood flow. Getting his thoughts back on track, this is what he had discovered: there was no Teddy in this world.

It hadn't taken him long to discover this fact. There was no record of him at Sussex university to start with. Cold trail. But he did have his semi-famous parents to rely on for more information. His father, Adam Coren, had existed. Following a life identical to the one Teddy knew well, he'd been a long standing lecturer at Bristol University, starting shortly after completing his PHD there and lecturing until his untimely death at forty-eight of a heart attack. Even the death date matched. His scientific articles were published in this world, just as they were in Teddy's, for everyone to see.

His mother, Elizabeth Rose Coren had also existed. A revered jazz musician, who in Teddy's world, later spent most of her evenings playing to a fatherless Teddy. The intricate piano trills fluttering like sorrowful birds in Teddy's young ears. The sorrow was felt in her playing, but Teddy never asked her to stop. It was as if they were holding hands through the vibrations in the air as she played.

But, *this* world's Elizabeth Rose hadn't had to play those sorrowful gigs to a little Teddy, because there never was a little Teddy. In fact, *Rose Rose*, as she had later become known, had gone on to record several more studio albums and even played at the Royal Albert Hall. This made Teddy both happy and sad, to think he might have been standing in the way of his mother's greatness.

Teddy silently mourned the death of these Corens as he had done in his world. He arrogantly scolded the fact that this world appeared to have functioned perfectly well without his existence. He contemplated the small effect the majority had on the world. But, Teddy knew his wings had grown substantially since his achievement, and he'd beat them until every peer, every institution that had doubted him, knew of his achievement. Until every parallel universe out there knew he was the greatest voyager in the cosmos. But, what his non-existence here had allowed him to do was the most important thing. It had allowed him to cross over. Teddy had only crossed over once, and he only had two pieces of evidence: his own walking talking body, and Adrian's dead body. For in *this* world, there was another Adrian Hoarding, easily found via a quick social media search in the library, his goofy grin beaming on his profile picture. Teddy's heart gave another heaving thud at the recent loss of *his* Adrian, but now it was laced with a pang of hope that he *would* be able to see him again, and as plans were currently forming, he would *have* to see him again. Teddy needed Adrian.

It seemed to Teddy that the universe, or universes, or whatever in Einstein sat above that, knew that skipping across universes was possible for its inhabitants. Like a little easter egg, hidden deep in a nebula a billion lightyears away. Teddy had surmised that although this sweet gift from the cosmos existed, no two beings from different universes may tread on the same world. It was only a theory, but he was the most qualified person to theorise this. It would explain the last few moments leading up to Adrian and Teddy crossing into this world perfectly. Teddy had been absolutely writhing to step through the bridge, foaming at the mouth like a wild animal. Adrian... Well the memories were foggy. He recalled a reluctance, as if something was warning him not to step through.

It's your fault. You pushed him through.

'Yes. Maybe I did.' Teddy wondered if he would have

acted any differently had he known what the consequences would be, but he knew the much greater cogs of the universe had been turning. Was it really his fault? His heart began to palpate.

So fucking what, it doesn't matter. There are infinite Adrians.

Something had snapped in Teddy. His perspective had changed. What importance did life other than his have? What was a life if it could be replaced in another world? There was a production line for him to pluck off. Teddy let out a deep breath and shuddered with satisfaction. His mind relaxed and the sound of blood squelching in his ear tapered off. He looked around and found that his legs had taken him down to the seafront. He sat down on a bench, pulled his jacket close around him and looked out to sea. Within moments, he'd once again forgotten that this wasn't his world.

18

'So, are we just going to doorstep Mrs. Turner then?' Bola said to Kim. It was the day after the report had come through and they'd now both read about Mr. Hoarding in full. Kim hadn't managed to resist. They both sat at their desks, chairs reclined, talking to the ceiling and letting their words bounce off the municipal panelling, which Kim was sure contained asbestos. Her throat started to tingle at the thought.

'I normally hate these situations,' Kim said.

'But?'

'But, something has been niggling me. It seemed like Mrs. Turner was at the mortuary for something else. Not as a wife, not as a widow. Almost like she was…' Kim struggled to find the words. Perhaps because she was still struggling to form the idea in her mind as well. All she knew is she wanted to follow up on it.

'Like she was checking in on something, like some sort of plan,' she said.

Kim slowly spun her chair around to Bola. She sat up

and adjusted her chair, correcting her posture after slouching. It felt good. She imagined her spinal discs stacking perfectly on top of each other like a fleshy totem pole.

'That might not be it, but I know the feeling, and it's one that I always follow up on,' she said.

'I'm in,' Bola said. 'Do we need to pretend we're there for something else?'

'Well, I can just play family liaison. Mrs. Turner shouldn't be too shocked at our arrival. After all, her husband was found dead and it's our job to find out how he got there. What she's probably expecting is a phone call though.'

'So, we don't call ahead. Is that a big deal?'

'At the moment, I feel morally wrong about dropping in unannounced. Not getting a slap from above.'

'I'm not telling.'

'I know you're not. But, if I've got this all wrong, it's not going to help with her mental state. We go in soft, just you and I. See how things are going, nothing too official.'

'We could be passing by?'

'We *could* be passing by, yes. It's a gamble but I don't think we're going to lose anything either way. I think it's worth applying a little stress to see if any cracks appear. That's all a bonus anyway; I do need to check on her.' Kim needed to convince herself a little more that this plan was actually morally sound. Bola nodded silently. It wasn't often that Kim did something like this, but she knew Bola wasn't necessarily adverse to going off-piste to get things done. The kiss on the forehead had certainly started to pull him around. Neither of them were trying to find clues left by ghosts; they were just hitting two birds with one hunch.

'Do we mention Marsh Avenue?' he asked

'In what regard? Just to see her reaction?'

'Well, kind of,' Bola surveyed his neatly arranged desk and plucked a few choice notes from a pile. 'I'd like to know if she's ever been up there, or knows where it is. It's a funny old street.'

'Oh?' Kim asked.

'Well, I've done some research and you've got to go back years to find anything, just domestic disturbances until...' She knew Bola was reeling her in. He already had her on the hook with this case, yet he loved giving her line a little tug here and there. She sat dead in the water not giving him the satisfaction, so he went on, unperturbed.

'Until Mr. Hoarding's death. Since then, we've had several calls about strange behaviour and one reported break-in. And it's infuriating no one passed on the reports and I had to go searching for them, we really need to get these workflows consolidated by the way.' Kim nodded in agreement, departments were always too busy with their own problems to talk.

'What's been happening?' she asked.

'People have been loitering outside the house.'

'Rubberneckers. And the break-in?'

'Ok, the *attempted* break-in was someone trying to get in the front door, which of course, is locked. They weren't even being sneaky about it.'

'Who were they?'

'No idea,' Bola said.

'Did any of our officers speak to anyone? Who reported it?'

'It was a neighbour from a house opposite who made the calls. The officers only attended the supposed break-in;

they didn't talk to anyone. But no one thought to call me up and loop me in. The officers just put it down to nosey neighbours, and didn't canvas the whole street. Odd though, right? All this activity?'

'After a murder people can get twitchy.' Again, Kim tried to let Bola get on with it. Sensing this, Bola got back to the topic of Mrs. Turner.

'You want me to keep an eye on anything while you're with Mrs. Turner?' he asked.

'No. Not at this stage. We won't be digging. We're just seeing how she reacts and we'll go from there.'

'We're searching *her* really then?'

Bola had hit the nail on the head. The tugging on Kim's gut wasn't about a hidden clue she'd missed; it was uncertainty about the suspects. They had a pretty blank slate at the moment. All they had was a dead body with no criminal record, in a house with no forced entry. Kim just wanted a bit more time with Mrs. Turner to put her mind at rest. Away from dead bodies and in a place where Mrs. Turner felt safe – her own home. Kim wasn't trying to make things stick that wouldn't stick, but striking Mrs. Turner from the investigation would be progress, nonetheless.

'We are. We still need to tidy things up at her end, anyway, get more background on Mr. Hoarding. Maybe even find out why she didn't take his last name. Were they progressive, or did she never really love him? Short-term marriage.'

'Wow. Harsh.' Bola said.

'I'm a bitch, aren't I? I don't think she'll let anything slip, even if she does know something. She seems to be pretty sharp, but she doesn't seem like a killer.'

'The good ones never do.'

Kim nodded. She spun slowly on her chair, reclined it, and stared back up at the ceiling letting her thoughts wander again. It took less than a minute for her throat to start scratching. She needed a new thinking pose. It was the same thought she'd had for years.

19

Caz pulled the car up two roads back from Marsh Avenue and killed the engine. It was three thirty in the morning and rain was being squeezed out from the invisible clouds that hung overhead, the heavy droplets peppering the roof.

She recalled driving up to the top of the Downs alone, a few days before what she had coined *D-Day*, to get her fix of blue skies somewhere on the horizon. Unfortunately, she was met with the same homogenous canopy draping over the horizon, no matter where she looked. The only sunny day recently had been D-Day but it now lacked warmth as the memories made it colder.

She turned to face Adrian who had come out of his hiding place in the boot and was now laying across the rear seats. She took in the state of her car. Empty single-use plastic bottles filled the footwell, sorry ocean; scrunched-up tissues full of tears and snot covered the dashboard, it had been an emotional few days; and empty crisp packets, chocolate and sweet wrappers filled the cubby holes in both doors. Again, it had been an emotional few days. A few extra heavy drops – the kind that pooled in the overhanging street trees – struck the roof of the car and they both squirmed.

'Ready?' Caz asked, gently.

'Sure. What could possibly go wrong?' Adrian replied. He was looking up through the window at the rain. 'Never broken into a house before, but how hard can it be? Apparently I've already managed it once. At least we know the owners are not home. Surely that's the typical complication for thieves?'

'Well, here's hoping. Are any… senses tingling?' Caz didn't really know what to say, this was a stupid idea. Caz had received a call from the police confirming that they had matched her supplied DNA samples to the body they had found. The man she had seen was a unequivocally Adrian Hoarding. Just not *her* Adrian Hoarding. Adrian and Mona's attitude had changed drastically since the "official" information and they were both apologetic about any doubts they had of Caz's identification skills. But now…Well who knew where they went from here? Nothing was off the table. Which is why they found themselves now sneaking out in the middle of the night looking for answers.

'No,' he said.

'Not really giving me much here, baby.'

'Sorry. Maybe I'm being stupid. I just feel like, if I was really here, something might ring a bell. Some kinda memory. For want of a better term, paranormal deja vu.'

Caz wondered if Adrian secretly wanted there to be some kind of hocus pocus answer to all of this. As if this wasn't already extraordinary enough. They had discussed clones, some kind of estranged twin or parallel universes. The estranged twin was taking the lead at the moment.

They had decided to check out the scene of the crime like a couple of television detectives, but hopefully not the type of detectives that are killed on site by a monster. Adrian's OCD had taken a turn for the worse after being cooped up in the house, and after two days of pacing around wearing out the carpets and creating new dances, they decided they had to do *something*.

Sitting there now, Caz felt like an idiot agreeing to this. She desperately wanted to turn the car back on and return home, sneaking Adrian out the boot again in the alley that ran behind their house. But, that wouldn't do. They were there after all, and each moment that passed and they didn't phone the police, the worse they made things for themselves. Maybe it was already too late to come clean with no consequences?

Seeing she would have to take the lead, Caz pulled up her hood, opened the door and stepped out of the car. The rain was just as hard as the car roof had indicated. Caz was no expert, but this seemed like perfect breaking and entering weather. No one would want to be walking around in this, and the rural area didn't have streetlights. After a moment, Adrian followed. He hadn't put his hood up in the car and was now struggling with it while the rain struck his face. After realising it was too tight with his zipper all the way up, he fumbled the zip down, flicked his hood up, zipped up, then spun to meet Caz's gaze with a toothy smile on his face. Clearly, he was happy to be out.

He's a wally, but I do love this man.

As they trudged through the rain, it soon became clear

they could have parked closer. Two roads didn't seem that far back on the online map, but down on the street these country lanes seemed never ending, and while Caz's waterproof shielded her head and torso, she could feel the rain soaking her jeans. They approached Marsh Avenue and slowed to locate the back alley they had seen online. It was hard to distinguish the narrow residential driveways from the alley they were after, and beneath all of this, Caz could hear her heart hammering inside her waterproof.

She felt Adrian's hand on the small of her back, and shortly after, his shoulder on hers. Caz let Adrian guide her between two hedges that had been stripped by the bitter winter and soon felt the ground beneath her change from pavement to slippery mud. They took a short break behind a large tree trunk a few metres in.

'It's on the left, the fancy house, between the two bungalows,' Adrian said in her ear. Caz nodded. On they went, counting the odd gardens. One, three, five - a little slip in the mud - seven. When they reached the rear of the property, Caz was glad to see the garden was well sheltered from prying eyes. Adrian gave the back gate a light push but it didn't budge. Without so much as a pause Adrian bent down and grabbed her legs. Before she knew it, her head was poking over the top of the wall. She took some weight with her hands; the brick top was wet and slimy. Adrian, feeling her weight shift, released one of her legs and readjusted his grip to the soles of her muddy boots. She briefly straddled the wall then let herself down in a similar fashion, allowing her feet to dangle briefly until they met something that felt like grass.

Thank god it's a short wall.

She spun around and squinted into the darkness, the

outline of the house visible from the end of the garden. A short scuffle later, Adrian landed beside her.

'Short wall ain't it?' he asked.

'At least our rock climbing is finally coming into some practical use.'

'Well, I'd always planned to advance into trespassing.'

Caz pointed out a sheltered path down the side of the garden. Adrian nodded and they shuffled across. The rain softened somewhat as it struggled to penetrate the long, manicured archway of conifers. No one could see into the garden as it was, but the extra precaution made sense. She turned to Adrian.

'Anything ringing some ghostly bells?' she quipped, still unconvinced there might be anything paranormal about their situation, unlike her husband.

'No, darling, you can put your Aurascope away.

'My what?'

'Never mind.' Adrian looked around the garden.

'I mean, I can hardly make anything out between the rain and darkness. But *I've* definitely never been here before. As in, me me.'

'Don't be a dick. You were the one that suggested some kind of paranormal event may be happening here, not me.'

'I'm not denying that, but I've no idea what to look for, even if that was the case. You're making me feel like an idiot, so let's just agree you stop asking me. I'll let you know if I get any tingles,' he said. Caz bit her tongue.

There were bi-fold doors set just off centre, and a double window on the right hand side. She peeked through the doors, giving up almost immediately, as she was unable to see inside. It was so dark she couldn't bring anything into clarity. It could have been a gateway to hell for all she knew. Adrian appeared to her side and immediately tried the door. It didn't budge.

Caz moved to the windows where she had a little more luck. She could make out a glint of something chrome that had managed to catch what little light there was. She cupped her hands around her face to aid with the task.

Kitchen tap?

Frankly, she didn't know what she was looking for, but she had a very odd feeling in her stomach, as if deep down she knew there was something to be found. Or was she just overtired and clutching at straws? The past few days had certainly been the hardest of her life. She'd had a ride on the emotional rollercoaster of loss, shed more tears than she thought she had fluid in her body for, and sleep wasn't coming easily. She was mostly worried that Adrian's murderer was still out there looking to get a complete set. *I'm just tired*, she thought, as the rain continued to wash over her. She pushed her feelings aside and went to return to Adrian, but stopped in her tracks. He hadn't moved from the door. Something was off. He stood dead still, one hand on the door handle where he had jokingly tried to get in.

'Adrian?' she said. He slowly turned his head to her but continued to clutch the door handle.

'I think… something is… here?'

A shiver enveloped her body and her stomach gave a physical lurch. She stifled a burp. Adrian looked at her with a very odd smile on his face. He looked a bit unhinged.

'Adrian, let go of the handle.' Adrian looked down to his hand and seemed surprised to find he was still clasping the handle. He recoiled as if it was suddenly ablaze, took a few steps back leading him off the firm patio and slipped on the sodden grass. He floundered on his feet, clutching at the raindrops, but ultimately gravity won and brought the rest of his body down to meet the sludge. Caz crossed the patio quickly, paying attention to her steps so as not to join Adrian in his mud bath. He was cupping his right hand in his left as if he really had burnt it.

'Adrian! Adrian, are you ok?'

'I… Yes, yes, I'm fine. I just… I was just shocked.'

Caz let out a gasp.

'No, I mean, that I was still clutching the handle, I wasn't electrically shocked. I just lost myself for a moment. I'm fine.'

She gave Adrian a hand from her safe anchor on the patio and he scrambled up. They both turned to look at the doors and the bottomless darkness behind them. The feeling that there was something to be found had once again left her stomach. She couldn't quite remember the feeling; it had barely left so much as a footprint. She turned once again to Adrian and he seemed to register the question on her face.

'No. It's gone. Fuck, I swear I felt something. Like, oh, it's like when…'

'A dream? When you wake up and the details start fading?' Caz answered, instinctively. It was almost as if they'd had shared an experience, but one they couldn't quite comprehend.

'This is ridiculous,' she decided. 'Adrian, let's just get out of here. It's too dark, this rain is impossible, and short of breaking in, I think we might have got what we came for.'

'We could break in?'

'I hope you're joking?' He didn't reply. She pulled him off towards the path without any resistance. Neither of them looked back.

Caz let herself down the other side of the wall as before, legs feeling for the ground, and landed back in the alleyway. She took a step back and saw Adrian's hands appear, followed by his head, then his whole body. When he was halfway over, she turned her head towards the end of the alley, expecting to see nothing, given the late hour and depth of the darkness, but her eyes managed to make out a figure where the alley met the road. Her body flushed with an icy panic. It didn't move.

Was it a tree?

She recalled the one they had briefly stood behind. She relaxed at this thought, but when Adrian dropped down from the wall to the alleyway: the tree moved. She let out a little scream.

'What?' He looked down the alley.

'Oh, fuck,' he said.

The rain hammered down on all three of them.

The figure had his shoulders hunched up against the rain. They shuffled a little, as if to approach them. Caz shot her hand out and found Adrian's arm, then squeezed it, hard. The figure hesitated. What if this was the guy who had killed the other Adrian? What if he was there to finish the job?

Fuck, fuck, fuck.

Just as these thoughts whizzed into Caz's already troubled head, the figure spun on their heels and made off up the road. Adrian and Caz both stood there while the rain continued to beat down on them both. She was absolutely soaked through. Caz blinked a few times and saw the faint silhouette of the figure had burned into her retinas, each flash frame sending a fresh shiver through her body. Finally, Adrian broke his trance and turned to face Caz.

'Who the fuck was that?'

20

Bola pressed the doorbell of Mrs. Turner's house and stepped back off the porch so as not to seem too intrusive. This was just a "courtesy call" after all. It appeared that Mrs. Turner had now installed a video doorbell and it was working - its LED light had flicked on. He knew this was a new addition from his last visit, even though he had been preoccupied with nerves on account of telling someone their spouse was dead.

He took in more of the house while they waited. Likely a nineteen-thirties build. It sat at the end of the terrace and blended in with the rest of the residential street. The street itself ran parallel with the main seafront road - the sound of cars along the main strip was present, the lapping waves were not. The houses on either side gave nothing of note and the alley between them looked well used. It was just another homogeneous row of houses that lacked imagination. Focusing once again on the house, Bola also noticed an additional security camera, placed just above the door with a wire feeding down into the porch tiling.

Looking further up he saw an alarm system placed in clear view between the two front windows. He turned to Kim who had apparently clocked all these additions too.

'All of this new?' he said.

'Yeah. I don't recall seeing it last time.' She motioned him over with her head, away from the video doorbell. 'Get on Street View when we get back.'

'Recently widowed,' Bola said, aware that these new doorbells could receive sound. 'Living alone. Unsure as to the cause of her husband's death. Not unusual to want a little more protection.'

Kim casually turned to look down the street, throwing her voice. 'Ensuring she's not taken by surprise?' They exchanged a glance and Kim swivelled back to the house.

With each day that passed Kim suspected Mrs. Turner knew more than she was letting on, and she wasn't being shy about it. Bola didn't even have a toe onboard that ship, yet. He still held the belief that although it was a suspicious death, Mrs. Turner wasn't involved. Her phone location had been static at this house on the night – not conclusive but helpful. She also had the alibi of her car being in the driveway that evening, witnessed by one neighbour – again, not conclusive but helpful.

Bola rapped his knuckles on the front room window. He lingered a little and inspected the closed blinds for movement, then looked back to the street. There was a low wall in the front garden, easy for passers-by to look in. He didn't think it too odd that they were closed in the middle of the day. He lingered a little longer, this time using his ears for reconnaissance rather than his eyes. A robin released chirps nearby while the cars down by the promenade continued to hum. He turned back to Kim who had taken a few steps back and was looking at the first floor windows for signs of life. Just over her shoulder he saw a curtain twitch, from the very same house that Mrs. Turner's alibi resided in. He made a mental note to bolster Mrs. Turner's alibi.

'Well, looks like Mrs. Turner is out,' Bola said, returning to a normal volume.

'I do hope she's doing ok,' Kim said a little louder than needed. 'I can't think how hard it must be. Perhaps you could return tomorrow?'

'Sure.' Bola wasn't quite sure where Kim was going with this, but played along.

'I'll be busy.'

'Yes boss. I'll make sure she's ok.'

Surely, Caz wouldn't go for this?

Kim turned on her heels and made her way back to Bola's car. He took one last look at the house, then followed. He couldn't believe it when he heard the crackle come through the doorbell.

'Hello?' The distorted voice stopped him in his tracks.

'Sorry, officers. I was just in the bathroom. I'll come down now.'

Bola went to give Kim the "nice job" eyes, but she had her game face on now.

No more fucking around.

After a moment, Bola started to hear various metallic noises on the other side of the door, then Mrs. Turner's face appeared.

It was in that moment Bola's needle started to tick over to the guilty side of the gauge. Mrs. Turner looked tired, sure, but there was something off, and it wasn't a piece of her heart – more the lack of a broken heart. Her eyes darted between them both, giving her the look of a cornered animal. Yes, this was an unscheduled visit, but she shouldn't have anything to hide. She broke the silence.

'Sorry. Bathroom.' Her tone was slightly flat and defeated. Bola went to flick his needle back into the innocent portion of his gauge but some internal mechanics didn't allow him to.

'Caz, how are you?' Kim asked.

She didn't seem to struggle so much for the words. Instead, it felt more like she didn't want to say them. Both Bola and Kim nodded politely at her silence.

'Well, we didn't want to disturb you. We were just driving back to the station along the promenade and thought we'd stop by. I hope that's ok? You don't mind us turning up out the blue?'

'Not at all,' she said.

'Good. How have you been getting on in the house?' Kim asked.

More animated faces of not being able to find the words, from Mrs. Turner.

'I see you've installed some extra security. That's understandable, darling. Are you worried at all?'

'No. I just. You know. My sister convinced me to,' Caz said.

Bola was in awe of Kim's handy work. It was like trying to get a fish onto a hook. A little give, a little take. Make them come to you; don't jump in with a spear.

'Well, she sounds like a smart lady. I'm sure everything is fine at home though. You've a very nice street. Nothing to worry about, I'm sure.'

'It is a good street.' Mrs. Turner let her eyes wander

past them to number four across the road, where her alibi lived.

'And your sister? She's ok?' Kim asked.

'Yes. She's been great.'

'Good, good. Is she with you now, you two weren't having a cup of tea?'

'No, she's back at work. Teacher and all that. She'll be back soon I imagine.'

'So, no tea then?' Kim asked with a smile. Caz seemed to make a quick decision, although not happily it seemed. She might genuinely not want anyone over. Kim was good but was she pushing it?

'Would you like tea, officers?'

'Oh, that would be lovely, darling. But, unfortunately, we've got to get back. Thank you for the offer though.'

Bola realised straight away what Kim had done. She was just seeing if the invitation was there. He found it hard to read Mrs. Turner's face at this rapid turn of events.

'Oh, right.' Caz replied.

'Honestly, you won't hesitate to call us if you need anything? I hope the DNA results help to, settle things.

'They are. I was just being silly.'

'Not at all, darling.'

Silence hung in the air and Bola wasn't too sure if he was the only one that felt awkward - but what happened next certainly did cause awkwardness.

'Ah, that's my sister now. Mona.'

They all turned, thankful for the distraction. Bola watched as a woman sheepishly walked up the drive. She looked oddly familiar to Bola, and not just because of her similarities to Mrs. Turner.

Mona?

The report had said *Ramona*. His mind tried to quickly place her.

'Hello,' she said as she reached them at the door. 'Bola?'

Shit! That Mona.

'Mona. Hi!' he said.

'Hi.' She smiled at him.

Bola watched Kim and Caz in his peripherals - they might as well be watching a tennis match.

'You know each other?' Kim asked.

'Yes. Yes we do.' He smiled, his cheeks likely flushing.

Bola and Mona had met just once before. It was on his very first night out in Furlong, just over a year ago. The encounter had gone well. Very well indeed. But at the time he still happened to have been in a relationship with his now ex-girlfriend, who lived in Manchester. They hadn't even exchanged details in the morning and Bola presumed she might have also been unfaithful to an unseen party that night. Bola's mind raced at the implications of this - he couldn't have a romantic history with a suspects sibling. He'd be pulled off the case.

'We met in a bar once. You'd just moved down if I recall?' she said.

'Yup. That's right. Manchester.'

'Oh yes. That's right,' Mona then looked to her sister and her smile faded.

'Sorry. Not the time for reunions. I've interrupted something.' Mona said.

'No, not at all. We were just leaving. We were just stopping by to check in. Do take care of your sister and don't hesitate to call. Any time.' Kim smiled at them both then nodded at Bola to wrap it up.

'Take care,' Bola quickly said, and followed on to his car.

'Thank you,' Mrs. Turner replied, a little stunned.

Bola started up his car and drove away from the house. As they hit the seafront promenade, Kim opened her mouth.

'Do I need to pull you off this?

'No.'

'It happened just after you moved down?'

'Yes.'

'Nothing since?'

'No. That was the first time I've seen her since.'

'I think even the neighbours could tell that. I don't have the resources to take you off this, Bola.' Kim suddenly pointed to some parking spaces on the side of the road.

'Pull over,' she said.

Fuck.

Bola did as he was told.

'I still want this case, Kim. It was a one night stand. I'm sorry, I should have put the pieces together. Ramona, Mona. It was a long time ago.' Kim gave him a very stern look then smiled.

'Don't worry. It's still yours.'

'Then why did you—'

'Because I want to hear all about it, obviously.' She unbuckled and got out of the car. Bola looked around to see they had pulled up outside one of the promenade bars. He looked down at his watch. It was nearly five o'clock.

'Fair enough.'

Bola waved Kim out of the bar as she grabbed her taxi. One drink had turned into two, two into three and a burger. It had been nice to catch up with Kim outside of work. Kim was fond of a beverage, but Bola got the sense she preferred to do it alone. She rarely joined for post work drinks. He headed to the toilets and pondered whether he'd also get a taxi or walk. He was unable to walk straight into the toilets and hadn't really noticed that the bar had become so busy - evidently they'd been rather lost in conversation around Mona and the case. The queue went down and eventually he found himself at the urinals between two friends who were loudly talking to each other, completely ignoring his presence.

'No fucking way am I getting the next round. It's Simon's round next.'

'We'll be waiting all night for him to pull his finger out.'

'Ha! Might as well have a bump of coke then.'

'Shhhhh!' One of the men eyed Bola up.

'What?' The other turned to Bola too. 'Oh you don't mind, do ya mate?' he said, tapping his own nose. Bola couldn't see any evidence of cocaine around his nostrils and he didn't want to wait around to see if he had any elsewhere on his person.

'Don't mind me,' he replied and made his way over to the sink. There was too much petty crime in this little town to bother with and Bola had no issues with idiots like that damaging their brains further. Bola watched the men as they lingered by one of the occupied cubicles. One started to fiddle in his pocket and the other looked round with a dumb smirk on his face and saw Bola watching.

'What?' The mouthier of the two said.

'Nothing,' Bola said, already imagining the feel of the man's face under his knuckles.

'Prick,' he replied.

Luckily Bola was only three drinks down, so the new image of grabbing the man's head and slamming it into the tiled wall over and over stayed safely in his head - for now. He had to tell both his feet to move out of the bathroom before one went searching for a knee cap. His impulsive nature had somewhat quelled since moving down to Furlong, but it still bubbled. The triggers down here didn't seem to stack as dangerously as they had in Manchester; perhaps it was the sea air, perhaps the constriction of city life had faded off him, or perhaps he had just grown up. The last impulsive thing he had done was Mona - literally.

Maybe I should be more impulsive?

With tipsy thoughts of Mona swimming through his head Bola thought he was imagining things when he bumped into the real thing outside the bathrooms. His stomach twinged and his crotch throbbed.

'Hello again,' he said.

'Are you following me, officer?' she said with a smile.

He gave his condolences; she said it was hard but they were doing ok. He stayed for a fourth.

He apologised for his lack of communication after their fling; she said there was nothing to apologise for - they were both adults.

A fifth.

He finally ordered that taxi - for two.

The sixth, was shared back at his house.

21

Adrian was playing with the cut on the side of his head. It had formed a nice crisp ridge during the past few days and he enjoyed running his finger along it. He was getting rather obsessed with it, seeing as there was nothing else to do - another dance to add to his repertoire. Unfortunately neither the small dose of mushrooms or the whack round the head had done anything to resettle his brain structure. The OCD wasn't going anywhere. It was just getting worse cooped up and playing dead.

He had been mindlessly staring at the TV in their spare bedroom, the screen judgingly asking if he was even still watching. Caz came into the room with Adriam's small suitcase and his suit bag. He looked at his neatly arranged city stickers and wondered if he'd ever make it out the country again.

'Off on hollibobs, are we?' he said. 'I was wondering when I'd get my "sorry for walloping you round the head" present. I see I'll be needing my suit. Fancy.'

'Yes sir,' Caz said with a thick Yankie accent. 'I'm

taking you to Neeeew York Citay!' She smiled, then placed the luggage aside.

'They're actually just your clothes. One way trip.'

Adrian was confused. Was this still part of the joke? She'd dropped her accent. His face clearly showed his confusion, so she went on.

'Well,' Caz started a little sheepishly. 'Your suitcase is full of clothes I never see you wear anymore, or that smell musty enough to indicate they haven't been worn.'

'Right,' he replied, still confused.

'And the other. The other is your suit for the funeral.'

'Jesus, fucking Christ, Caz.'

'What?'

'That's a bit... *strong* isn't it?'

'Adrian, when people die, they have a funeral. The police are done with that body now and the funeral directors are in charge. Don't forget, it's not actually you! That said, we need to start acting like you're really dead. At least *I* need to start acting like that. Who knows who that was the other night. They seemed to be there for a reason, no one goes for a stroll at that hour. And what if those detectives had come inside? How quiet could you have stayed, upstairs in the attic? That wasn't a courtesy call. I'm a suspect in *your* murder. They might think I killed you for some kind of pay-out. We need to keep this ship moving for both the murderer and the police now. We're too deep and we still need to figure out how to bring you back to the land of the living one day. We can't go on like this. And no, we're not claiming your life insurance before you ask.'

'Pffffft. At least...' Adrian knew he didn't really have any defence here. Caz was smart. If she ever did commit a crime, the police would have a hard time pinning it on her. Admitting defeat, he turned to his only one reliable tool, humour.

'That's my good bloody suit and you want to go drape it on Dead Dave.'

'And what will everyone say if they see I've put you in a cheap suit? Especially the police.'

'Who's going to see me through the coffin?'

'Adrian, you didn't feel the tension when they were talking to me.'

'I heard some of it from the attic.'

'No Adrian. You didn't *feel* it. The way they were snooping around. They know something is up. They'll be back.'

'And the suitcase is for…'

'Only for a little while. Until we figure this out. What if they really do come back, but this time with a warrant.'

'Where am I going to go?'

'Mona's.'

'Oh. That's not actually a bad idea.'

'I know. Mona and I already chatted. It will be another night drive in the boot for you.'

'Becoming quite the criminal team aren't we?'

'The faster we find out who did this, and what the hell is going on, the faster we can get back to normal life.' Caz breathed out an exhausted sigh.

'Have you thought what that normal will look like yet? I've been trying to carve out some scenarios but I keep finding more issues. How do we even go about telling everyone that I'm not actually dead, authorities and all? I'm going to be buried in a couple of days, or burnt.' Caz winced at Adrian's words.

'Sorry, Dead Dave will be buried or burnt.' Caz still winced.

They had spoken about this at length and couldn't come to a decision on what the best way to deal with Dave's body was. Burying seemed like the sensible option, then when it came to bringing this all out in the open they had a body to go back to and some physical evidence that there were indeed two Adrian's. However, at this, he also felt pangs of fear that both he and Dave would be carted off to some secret testing facility to get to the bottom of what had happened.

Cremation brought its own whacky fears. Mainly, the panic he felt at the thought of another version of him lying in a matchbox with one thousand degree flames licking at the body. What if he started to burn also? He didn't know what the connection was between them yet. He suddenly felt very warm.

They had continued spit balling whacky theories since the police had confirmed via DNA sample that Dave was Adrian – no mistaking. So, where did he come from? The clone theory was gaining some weight, but who would waste resources cloning him? A delightfully refreshing theory was that an alien imposter had stolen Adrian's DNA when he'd urinated on a bush one day. More than anything, he wished they'd told the truth at the start.

'Maybe we *should* go to New York City,' Caz said, interrupting his thoughts. 'Get far away from here and start a new life where no one knows you're dead. America seems like an easy place to disappear to. Maybe the airports don't know you're dead yet, I don't know how this information travels.'

'Or, maybe I could squeeze into our big suitcase and

you won't even need to pay for the flight?' Adrian suggested.

'Flight?' Caz put her hands on her hips theatrically, Yankie accent back in play. 'It'll be a cruise liner for us. Say, we'll sail into the sunset together with your life insurance money. Hey, that's a pretty swell idea, huh?'

They both giggled. Amongst all this shit, they were managing to cling onto their sense of humour, one of the renewable fuels of their marriage. Adrian lifted his arm and Caz came over to tuck herself under it. Her head had barely touched his chest when there was a knock at the front door. Adrian froze while Caz sprang away from his chest. They both looked at each other wide eyed, then towards the clock. It was nearly eight p.m.

'Shit. The police are back already,' she said.

'Can they get a warrant that quickly?' Adrian was already up and heading towards the attic steps - they'd kept them constantly down.

'I don't know. Probably. They're the police, and I'm rapidly turning into suspect number one, clearly.'

'Well, maybe this is where we tell them?' Adrian suggested, stopping halfway up the steps. Caz looked helplessly at him.

'They can't arrest you if I'm still alive,' he said.

'But—' she started. Adrian saw Caz's cogs whirling, thinking through all the possible outcomes. Were they too deep to swim ashore? Adrian came back down and put his hands on her shoulders.

'Maybe it's time. Maybe there is no murderer.'

'Are you sure? But in the alley? I just don't know what to do anymore. What is going on? We were just suggesting that running to the States might not be the worst idea.'

Caz's phone vibrated in her pocket. Whoever was at the door had pressed their video doorbell. She went to pull it out but Adrian stopped her. He was prepared to meet his fate, whatever that might look like. He hoped the police wouldn't come down too harshly on Caz.

'It's time.' Adrian felt tears coming. All the emotions of the past few days came bubbling to the surface. He felt the release was near.

'Ok,' Caz said.

'Let me go. The shock might help them understand what we've been going through.' He pulled Caz in close and planted a kiss on her head.

'It's going to be alright,' he said, then headed down.

Someone seemed to have added an extra flight of stairs; the trip down seemed to take longer than normal. Adrian slid the various bolts across, absently wondering if they would keep them on when all this was over. Behind him, he heard Caz reach the bottom of the stairs, pulling her phone out which was still angrily vibrating in her pocket at being ignored. They'd keep the fancy doorbell at least.

Just as Adrian opened up the door, Caz yelled from behind for him to stop, but it was too late. He'd swung it open at speed like he was ripping off a plaster to make it less painful. He wasn't immediately aware that the man he was faced with wasn't one of the detectives. It wasn't until the man spoke with tears in his eyes that Adrian realised it was not.

'Hello Adrian. I'm Teddy.'

22

'Adrian! Shut the bloody door,' Caz screamed as she looked at this stranger from the foot of the stairs. Adrian was frozen to the spot.

'No one killed Adrian there was an accident!' the man spurted out in a hurry, aware his time might be short. 'It's all my fault. Please, if you'll let me explain.'

'Just shut the door!' Caz repeated.

Adrian awoke from his daze and went to shut the door but he was too slow. The man skipped inside with a surprising amount of dexterity for his age then clumsily laid down on the hallway floor, wincing as he went.

'What the hell?' Adrian said.

'I just want to show you I'm no threat. Please.'

Caz looked down, stunned at this bizarre turn of events. They had been on the cusp of coming clean with the police and they now had a man submissively lying in their hallway.

'Just shut the fucking door,' Caz said one last time. Adrian shut the door but didn't tend to the bolts.

Their secret was out. This man lying on the floor was the first person to know Adrian was still alive apart from Mona. She studied him hard so as to take in every detail and be on the lookout for any duplicity. He was a slight, older man, and in the artificial light of the hallway, his years seemed even more advanced. On his gaunt neck perched a round face with reddened cheeks. He didn't look like your average murderer, but then who did? Caz actually fancied her chances against him if it got physical. His most striking feature, although perhaps temporary, was the sheer look of tiredness on his face. Like he'd been subjected to an arduous journey he had not quite recovered from. He wore hiking boots, blue denim jeans and a grey lumber shirt. She looked down at a bague ripstop satchel he was carrying.

What was in that?

'Who are you?' Adrian asked, now fully alert.

'My name is Teddy Coren. I'm a scientist and I can explain everything.'

'Go on then,' Caz said, standing over him now.

'Well, it's quite a long story.'

'And?' she said.

'Well, might I get up?'

Caz looked at Adrian to silently assess the situation, but rather unhelpfully, he shrugged his shoulders. Caz didn't want to give away their advantage but she was sure a hard tiled floor wouldn't be good for someone of his age.

'Fine. But leave that satchel,' she said.

'Of course, thank you.' The man got to his knees then looked at them both, slightly embarrassed.

'Might I have a hand?' he said.

Adrian apologised and helped Teddy up. Caz wasn't

sure why Adrian was apologising, but she was distracted by the way the man seemed to hold on a bit too long after he had his footing, almost as if he was lingering near Adrian. She tried to get a read on his face but he quickly buried it in a shaking hand.

'Nice to meet you both,' he finally said.

Adrian returned a confused stare, squinting in an attempt to place the man. Teddy turned his gaze to Caz, less enthusiastically, but still a nine out of ten if she had to measure it.

'Come through,' Adrian offered.

Caz whipped around to give Adrian a face full of scorn but he'd already proceeded through, and Teddy was hot on his heels. She was momentarily left alone and stunned in her own hallway when the sound of the kettle clicking on brought her to.

Tea? Are you fucking joking, Adrian?

She stopped briefly at the cupboard under the stairs. The door was ajar. The cupboard mainly served as storage, but a few of the more frequently used tools were stored there as well; chiefly, the hammer and screwdrivers. Without a second thought she grabbed the flathead screwdriver and popped it into the front joey pocket of her denim dungarees. She walked slowly into the room, closed the door behind her and took up a position a couple of metres behind Teddy.

The kettle clicked off and Adrian poured boiling water into the three mismatched mugs laid out on the worktop. He gave them a quick stir, added some oat milk, gave them another quick stir and removed the bags. Adrian's not all there, Caz thought. That was the quickest tea she'd ever seen him make. He normally obsessed over every detail when making tea. It was a ritual for him. He took the first mug, with a faded "Congratulations" dully printed on the side, and handed it to Teddy, who thanked him warmly. Adrian took up the other two mugs, walked past Teddy without a word and handed it to Caz. He looked into Caz's eyes. The confusion had gone, replaced with love and reassurance. He lifted his hand and cupped her cheek, it was still warm from holding the mug. She leant into it and relaxed a little.

As Adrian left her field of vision, Teddy came into view. His eyes fixed on Caz's and for the briefest moment she thought she saw jealousy in them. Teddy smiled, gave his tea a blow and walked over to join them.

23

Teddy thought it best to start with his background. He didn't want to open at the twist. Adrian stared at Teddy with no sense of recognition. His heart bubbled in sadness.

'I'm a scientist – a theoretical physicist. Or at least I...Never mind. My work has moved slowly through different areas over the years and as you can see, it's been many years. Astrology, cosmology, quantum theory, jack of all, master of none. I've hopped across universities, so my work tends to change with the needs of the curriculum.'

Teddy paid attention to Adrian throughout this sentence. He leaned forward a little, almost imperceptibly, and his eyes had become more attentive. He'd nibbled on the carrot, *this* Adrian was also interested in science. They might well be similar, unlike some other things in this world. Caz seemed to be following but didn't necessarily seem intrigued.

'I published the odd article here and there, nothing special. All theoretical. Some thought them outlandish.

Anyway, I kept myself busy with research, all the while working on my own projects when I could.'

Life as a relief lecturer could have been busier. Teddy was mainly called by the desperate in need of a cheap mind. He often got lost in his own work. Caz took this opportunity to interrupt his thoughts.

'Sorry. We really don't care about this,' she said. 'While I'm guessing you're trying to win our trust, I – we – want to know how you knew Adrian was alive, and who the fuck that other man was, because *this* is Adrian.' Adrian calmly placed a hand on Caz's thigh. It didn't go down well.

'No, Adrian,' she shot back, rising to her feet.

'When have we ever let someone into this house who randomly knocks on our door? Secondly, why on Earth did you decide today was that day? Stop being so fucking calm about this and don't try and make me calm by acting calm because it's winding me the fuck up. No one even asked for tea.'

My God, she's got a gutter mouth, Teddy thought.

'Do you know who this is, Adrian?' Caz said, as Teddy sat there silently, but not uncomfortably. The more they fought, the better for his plans. Adrian looked to Teddy slowly, then back to Caz.

'I don't know him, Caz. I've no idea who he is. Apparently, I'm meant to be dead. We haven't had anyone, not one person, not one police officer sniff around the fact it might not actually be me lying dead in that morgue. Because apparently it *is* me. You say so, they say so, the DNA says so.' Adrian's voice broke here. Like he was bemoaning his own death.

'I'm having nightmares of suddenly waking up in a

coffin. Like the universe forgot to put me and that body back together before it died. This man has clearly put himself in some danger by coming here and I'm quite sure you could take him if he kicks off.'

Caz placed her hands on her hips after Adrian's speech. She stood silently for a few seconds, bobbing her head with her tongue pushing out her bottom lip, then let her hands drop in resignation.

'Fine. Let's hear the rest of this shit, then.' She walked back through to the entrance hallway and out of sight. The sound of metal on metal was heard for a second, then she returned with a slightly rusted hammer. She placed the hammer down hard on the table, drilling home the weight it carried, picked up her tea, crossed her legs, smiled and took a sip.

She's a savage.

Adrian hadn't really done much in the way of questioning and had happily let Teddy into their house for a cup of tea - although Teddy did find it odd he hadn't let it brew. That wasn't like his Adrian at all, he thought. Teddy cleared his throat of the nerves that were creeping in.

'I assure you, I'm not here to hurt you.' He directed this to Caz more than Adrian. She held his gaze and widened her eyes, indicating he should get on with it.

'So, for the past two years I've been lucky enough to have a post at Sussex University, Astrophysics. Not far from here. I don't normally get a post for so long, but the old lecturer decided to extend her sabbatical so...' Caz questionably cocked her head at him again.

'Right, sorry. Probably don't need that much detail,' Teddy said. Caz smiled then took another menacing sip of her tea. He was very conscious of the fact this could all go wrong. What will they do – what will *she* do – when he tells them what's really going on? They could easily kill him once they knew. No one knew Teddy was alive – he didn't even exist in this world.

But why would they, the scientific part of him reasoned? He needed to get a handle on his emotions.

'Anyway, whilst there, I met a student. A mature student, retraining in theoretical physics. He was working on his master's thesis. Brilliant mind. He was full of ideas and theories, but not entirely sure where all the pieces went yet. His Maths wasn't great. Well, we got to talking and it turned out we made quite the team when it came to problem solving. I'd been working on a formula for...' Teddy chose to omit some details here, using Caz's rules as a loophole, 'science stuff, you know. He humorously suggested I try to work my problem out in something called quantum physics, not classical astrophysics. The reason this is funny is because they're literally worlds, well, galaxies, apart.'

Teddy giggled to himself and Adrian joined in lightly. Caz swivelled her head once more to Adrian. Teddy jumped on this before Caz could bring this train to a stop again.

'Do you know much about physics, Adrian?' Teddy said in his most approachable teaching voice. Caz's eyes were wide and Teddy sensed she wanted to weigh in.

'Well, do you, darling? Regular Einstein all of a sudden, are we?'

'Well, I've... I've read a book or two over the years.' Adrian sounded rather awkward admitting this to the room. Teddy could see why. That sort of thing can happen when somebody who has a hobby, is suddenly confronted by the real deal. Someone who lives and breathes what is just a pastime to them.

Science wasn't anything less than life for Teddy. He shared a bond with science, like nucleons in an atom. But things were going haywire, he needed his other proton back. Adrian continued.

'Nothing academic I don't think, more just pop literature. Although, a couple by Stephen Hawking. I chuckled because that kind of physics and quantum mechanics are different, one is big and one is small. Classical physics is about the objects we see, like Newton and the apple – big things. Quantum stuff is all tiny. As in, atoms, and then what makes them... subatomic. That's the word.' He quickly regrouped himself, curbing his enthusiasm.

Wow, Teddy thought. He really looked like *his* Adrian in that moment. A hungry student on a new path in life, truly seeing the fascination of the scientific world. Of course, this was Adrian, but he'd taken a different path. Sad.

'Very good, Adrian. That about summarises it for our needs here. So, ultimately, he helped me with his lateral thinking, I helped him with his course work. It was simple stuff really, and he managed to stay on afterwards snatching a Phd. I had a heavy hand in that – guilty, to say – but all in the name of science. You see, I needed him around as he'd really escalated my research, exponentially so, with his fresh, eager open mind. He often thought like a child. Not bound by consequence and responsibility, often fearless, due to not fully understanding the former. Feynman said, "science is just imagination in a straightjacket". Richard Feynman, famous scientist back in the day. Well, luckily, my prodigy's straightjacket didn't quite fit him yet. My research was far-fetched and I often thought it foolish. I'm not saying he had an answer to every problem we hit, or every question the universe has handed humanity, but we did make a good team.'

Caz cast a face of mild calculation at this. She seemed to be leaping ahead of Adrian to see where this was going, proving to be quite the volatile substance. She was quick. *His* Adrian had divorced *a* Caz Turner and hadn't spoken much about her. Teddy hadn't pried.

'And what was your research?' Adrian asked, genuine interest in his voice. 'You just said "science stuff" earlier.'

'Well, it is a mix of cosmology and quantum mechanics, as I said. But, more specifically, it's something within string theory and within that, brane. Without going into it, branes are objects which, in theory, can propagate through spacetime.' Teddy checked in on Adrian's conscripted pupils – no recognition. Adrian might not have paid as much attention to his books as he let on.

'Have either of you heard of string theory?' Teddy asked, casually, so as not to make a big thing of it. If he started talking about dimensions their minds might run away with them. They both shook their heads and looked at each other.

'Ok, well that's good. It's rather far-fetched. I suggest, for the moment, we leave it there and you can do a bit of light research before our next session. That's why I brought my bag along to make this simpler. Let me grab it.' Teddy placed his empty mug down and stood up.

'Woah, woah, woah.' Caz took to her feet and pulled out a screwdriver from her dungarees while flanking around to block the exit.

'Fucking hell,' Adrian said. 'When did you put that in there?'

She didn't respond. Teddy felt extremely vulnerable. He raised his hands slowly in surrender, then the thought of a screwdriver penetrating through his palm made him curl his fingers.

'I was just getting my bag,' Teddy said, his confidence waning. What else was she hiding in that pocket? He really wasn't good with confrontation outside of an argument about physics. He may not be tough, but he was smart.

'There are some complicated theories I need to explain, and it's no use me rattling these off if you're–'

'Stupid? Dumb? Ignorant?' Caz began listing with the point of the screwdriver. Teddy looked at Adrian.

'Uh, uh, don't you go to him for help. Eyes on me. What have I learnt in the past ten minutes? That you are some wandering physicist going from university to university, trying to scoop up a bit on the side? The way you spoke about your pupil, it was clear you were more than just research partners, and frankly, it felt like you were alluding to Adrian, but that's not possible, unless you meant the dead Adrian.' She gave him an unblinking stare.

Teddy had planned for them to read between the lines of what he'd said, but Caz had leaped right ahead. However, he could see she was missing a crucial piece of the puzzle. The how.

'I had the police at my door telling me my husband was dead. I saw *my* husband lying dead on a cold fucking gurney. *Twice.* We have been living in fear these past few days, thinking some murderer is on the loose, and should they see *this* Adrian, they'll think they missed, and kill him too. So, I'm not letting the only person who knows what's going on, waltz into my house, give me a prologue, then piss off.' Her eyes filled with tears but her voice didn't break. She was acutely focused. 'Oh, *and* drink my tea. Just tell us what is going on.'

'Look. I am very sorry about all of this. Truly. The confusion. We didn't plan for any of this to happen. I promise I am here to help you, but for the time being, all I can give you is my word. Nobody killed Adrian. There is no murderer. I'm still figuring this out. It's very important we don't rush this, that you allow me time to explain my research, and explain those feelings you might have felt the other night,'

'So that was you at Marsh Aven–' Adrian started but Teddy had to steamroll him.

'To help comprehend the much, much bigger picture. Not to protect me, but to protect you and your sanity. My background is physics, yes. But, as an unwanted aside, I am a lecturer. I'm used to conveying ideas in such a way that makes it simple enough for,' Teddy chose his words carefully here, 'someone who hasn't *studied* this field to understand. You need to digest the fact today that there are things in science that even scientists don't understand. Things so beautiful and terrifying that make you question your life, reality. That make you question if this is science or the work of some greater cosmological being.'

Teddy let the last of the breath in his lungs out. Adrian placed his cup of tea down, stood up, and took a step towards Teddy. Teddy's heart began to beat hard and fast. How had he managed to go this long in Adrian's presence without breaking down, without wanting to run over and embrace him? His musk…That sweet Adrian musk. It was intoxicating. He felt like he was smelling it for the very first time. Teddy struggled to meet Adrian's gaze until Adrian filled his view. It was unavoidable. They locked eyes and Teddy felt his legs begin to tremble.

He was hot. His stomach was crammed full of rampant butterflies eager to escape their sanctuary. He was sure that if he lifted his shirt and looked down, he would see his old wrinkled gut undulating from their flapping wings. Then Adrian raised his hand toward Teddy, as if to place a hand on his shoulder. This is it, Teddy thought. He wouldn't be able to hold it in. He'd let his emotions swarm. Grab him, embrace him, kiss him, smother him. But Teddy didn't melt, he simply popped and came back to his senses. For Adrian didn't place a calm reassuring hand on his shoulder like he had done so often in Teddy's world. He poked him. Popping him like a balloon, killing the butterflies with a vicious pesticide, making his legs as strong as two mature cedars. Adrian looked menacingly into Teddy's soul. Clearly, being a dead man walking had given him some spunk.

'Now *you* listen. We don't know what the fuck is going on, but we sure as hell want to know what is going on. I have been stuck in this house churning the facts over for days. Who would want to kill me? Why was I in that house? I've been angry with my wife, thinking she wrongly identified me, *twice*. I haven't told the police for fear the murderer will realise whoever they killed wasn't the real me, that they'll come back for seconds, finishing the job once and for all. You've just given me a free pass. There is no murderer. *That* I do believe, and if it was you, I'm not scared in the slightest. You *will* tell us the full story. If we don't get it, that's not our problem. You can then leave us alone, and we go on with our fucked up little lives and figure this out ourselves. Because, frankly, given the situation, I don't think much is going to surprise us.'

At that point, Teddy felt no connection with this Adrian. But he knew that feeling wouldn't last long.

'Look, Adrian–' Before Teddy saw it, Adrian had given him a firm shove, and he stumbled backwards into the wall.

Teddy was raging. Caz had done this to Adrian. She had made this barbarian. No wonder he'd left her. He looked Adrian dead in the eyes.

'I'm from a parallel universe. A parallel Earth.'

The words made absolutely no impact. Both Adrian and Caz were as still as wax models. For a second, Teddy wondered if they were even breathing. Had he just broken some inter-cosmic taboo he was unaware of? A sentence that would break a human just by being spoken? Slowly, Adrian's features shifted into some kind of understanding, but it quickly went away. Then, a word left his mouth, hoarsely. That one monosyllabic word that covered a thousand questions and could effectively hold a conversation in place, indefinitely.

'What?' Adrian said.

'There are two Adrian's. Hell, an infinite amount, theoretically. There are infinite Earths, in infinite universes, which are in infinite states. The Adrian you saw was one of them. He wasn't from *your* planet, solar system, galaxy or universe. He's from *mine*. I don't know why he died, I'm trying to figure a lot of stuff out. My bag. There's some literature, articles, some of my research. Read what you can before we next meet.' He was already heading to the door before he finished his sentence. Caz let him pass. Neither talked as he left, and he took it that his instruction landed. Would they run to the police now they knew there was no killer? He left with a final bombshell.

'You have to keep up appearances. Adrian must continue to be dead. You *must not* tell the police about this yet. The whole world could be in danger.'

That ought to do it.

He unlatched the door himself stepping out into the cold spring air. It felt like heaven to him after the pressure cooker that was the house.

24

Mona sensed her sister on the other side of the door, silently watching.

'It's me. Can't all your cameras tell you that?'

Mona had come straight from the school. It had just gone four p.m. when she finished cleaning the classroom from her last practical session and a notification on her phone changed her plans for the evening. She heard bolts slide on the other side of the door. Caz and Adrian were particular about house safety prior to all this nonsense, but since the unfortunate death of that man, they'd upped the ante of their precautions. They had installed the peep hole, two extra Yale security locks on top of the one they already had, two chains and a quarter-inch-thick deadbolt, on both the front and back doors of their house. Not to mention the security locks on the windows, an alarm system and motion detecting CCTV. A pretty penny. Once the final bolt had slid, Caz opened the door and ushered Mona in. She knew to move quickly in order to avoid her sister's scorns.

Mona kicked her shoes off and made her way into the dining room while Caz restored order to the front door. Adrian was halfway down the stairs – Caz must have told him it was safe. She did still think they were playing it a bit too casual inside their own house. What if someone did charge in behind Mona. She pushed this thought aside as she had more important issues to raise.

'Adrian. Quickly, get down here.'

'Ooh, this sounds exciting,' he said.

Mona found Adrian's positivity odd, but she thought with being cooped up in this house, his sources of entertainment were limited. Caz joined them just as Mona slipped her phone out of her pockets.

'So, you know I'm still looking for a house, yada yada yada?' They both knew of her ongoing plight on account of her picky nature, and nodded. 'I got a notification of a new listing today.'

'And you rushed here to tell us? What is it, Buckingham Palace?' Adrian quipped.

'I know you can't, but you really need to get out, Adrian.'

'That's fair,' he said. 'Continue.'

'Maybe just lie under an open window?' she suggested.

'Mona,' Caz interrupted. 'What is it?' Mona was taken aback by this snap from Caz. She looked at her sister properly and could tell something was up. She then looked at Adrian and saw the same look. Had they been arguing?

'What's happened?' Mona asked. Caz and Adrian looked at each other.

Oh no, what has happened?

'Yesterday–' Adrian started.

'Yesterday, Adrian was a fucking idiot and snuck out

the house,' Caz cut in. Adrian didn't react. 'We've been arguing is all.'

Mona was stunned by this. Out of the house, was he mad? She had a niggling feeling that wasn't the full story, or perhaps the story at all. But in her excitement, she couldn't be bothered to deal with their relationship issues if that's all it was.

'Marsh Avenue. It's for sale.' Caz and Adrian looked at each other again, but this time more engaged.

'The house?' Adrian asked.

'No. The whole avenue, Adrian. Yes, the house, you plum.'

'Woah, woah, alright. What's with the attitude?'

'Just, use your... Sorry. I'm just a bit flustered. The kids in my last session were a pain. This is important though. Things are cooling down, and more importantly...' She held her hands out for them to pop the cherry on the cake.

'We can get into the house,' Caz said.

'Yes! You two can get into the house if you want to try and figure something out,' Mona said.

'Well, no. *We*.' Caz gestured to Mona.

'We?' Mona thought she'd play dumb.

'Well, I can't walk in there with my dead husband, can I?'

'They won't know who you two are,' Mona said.

'Mona, have you heard of this thing called the internet, and its little rotten child: social media? I *might* be unknown, but whether I wanted it or not, Adrian's face is as familiar as the sun in the sky right now.'

Mona knew Caz was right and that thought had occurred to her while running over here. Now she thought of it, that was probably the main reason she came over here. She was letting herself get sucked into this madness - she *felt* the need to get involved. That annoying family bond that drags you to your sibling's side, even when you know they're in the wrong, that keeps you at your lonely grandparents when you'd rather be at home on the sofa and makes you say yes to babysitting while again, you'd rather be at home on the sofa, but with wine this time.

'I know,' Mona said. 'Of course I'll come.' Caz gave her a warm smile – the same smile Mona had seen all through their lives, and that was worth the world.

'I'll make an appointment. Should be alright to go in the next few days – if they let me view. You should see the thing inside, it is lush. Well out of my range, but I just like looking. You know me. Maybe we can play rich girls.'

'I bet most of the town will want to get in there just to have a look,' Adrian said. 'Just be careful.'

Mona half listened, but in truth she had drifted off into her own thoughts. She'd driven by 33 Marsh Avenue the other day, but hadn't told Adrian or Caz. She hadn't been up to Cable's Wood in years and was just plain curious. On her first pass she didn't get a good look – someone was standing outside the house with their dog. After a spin round the block, however, she had better luck and managed to slow to a crawl as she passed.

The house itself was beautiful; a skilfully executed conversion of an old generator store which, in a street of bungalows, should have stuck out like a sore thumb. But, somehow it worked. She admired the coils of wisteria now smartly trained around the lower window and door, cut back and ready to release their dormant energy onto spring. The front garden was landscaped, and flower beds held bulbs eager to burst, in symphony with the wisteria. It was all very inviting at first glance, but the longer she looked, the more uneasy she felt – sick almost. It wasn't until a beep issued from the car behind that she realised she was no longer crawling along, but idling in the middle of the rural street. She shivered at the memory.

'Mona?' Adrian asked from the kitchen. 'Tea?'

'Huh? Oh. No, I've got to get on. Thanks though.' Mona had to get onto something that she wasn't planning to share with Adrian or Caz: Bola Cassin. After playing ships in the night for over a year they had bumped into each other twice in one day. Much like the first time they had met, the conversation was easy. The sex, that was even better. Mona wondered if it was the situation that had made it more exciting, more breathtaking. Bola was heading over tonight and unfortunately it might be the last time for a while with Adrian moving in temporarily. She had been unable to say no to her sister's plea. How would it have gone down?

"Why *can't* Adrian move in for a while Mona?"

"Because I'm shagging the detective that's probably trying to pin a murder on you, sis."

"Oh, fair enough then."

She made her way to the hall and Caz placed a hand on her back.

'You don't have to come,' she said.

Mona smiled back, 'Come on, can't have you going without me.' She slipped her last trainer on. 'Besides, maybe I'll like the house. I am still looking, you know.'

'I know this is completely whacky. But–' That look returned to Caz's face once more, like she wanted to tell Mona something. Perhaps they were both keeping secrets.

'Caz? What is it?'

'Nothing. It's silly. We did feel something funny when we snuck into the garden. It would be good to know if that was caused by nerves.'

'You don't need to explain to me, Caz. I saw how you were when you thought Adrian was dead. I know you don't want to feel that again.'

'I *never* want to feel that again. I'll kill myself on *his* deathbed if it meant not feeling that again.'

'Stop it.'

'Thanks. Do you need a lift?'

'No, no. Gotta save the planet!'

They hugged, then Mona waited while Fort Knox was once again tackled. She broke into a light jog once she got down the street, stirring the butterflies that were inside for Bola. How had she got herself into this pickle, she might genuinely have a good thing going with Bola this time. Perhaps this might even help them?

No darling. This most certainly won't help anyone.

25

Steven Drellis wiped vomit from his mouth for the second time that day. A sick estate agent was a useless estate agent, he thought. His forehead was beaded with sweat and he felt more than a little bit lightheaded. On this occasion, he hadn't made it to the toilet. He was bent over, hands on his thighs, looking at the now-soiled soil at the front of number 33 Marsh Avenue. The air cooled his back through his sweat-stained shirt. He untucked his tie from the safety of his shirt buttons and it swung gently from foot to foot in the breeze. He followed it with his eyes. Left, right, left right.

Urgh, that's not helping.

He stood and raised his head to the sky, eyes closed. He drew a deep breath in, and the cold air prickled his lungs where his shallow breathing had made them dull. He was starting to feel better; being outside had helped. He levelled his head, opened his eyes and was met with the sight of an old lady standing near her bins at the house opposite, number 36. He recalled it last sold in 2016 for £437,500. He gingerly raised a hand and waved hello.

'You want to get home to bed, dear,' she croaked across the quiet road, then turned back up her drive, signalling the end of the interaction. He returned a smile to the back of her head and checked his watch – his "Rolex" – which he picked up at a questionable market in the south of Italy a few years back. It ticked not so smoothly along and told him it was nearly midday. He had a few minutes until the next viewing. He headed to his agency branded car, removed his tie and undid his top button on the way. He tossed his tie on top of his blazer in the front seat and thus became the most under-dressed estate agent in town. *Sharp suit, quick sal*e – a secret insight his first manager, Mr. Baumann, had passed onto him all those years ago.

Secret insight?

'More like, Estate Agent 101,' he said to himself.

He popped the glove compartment open and rummaged around for some paracetamol to help with his temperature, and came up with two blisters – one completely empty, and one containing a single tablet. He wondered at what stage the unspoken rule of two at a time had been broken, but he shrugged and slid one into his mouth and took some hearty gulps of water while looking back at the house.

Steven had refused to phone the office and tag out after his first bout of sickness. The house was hot property, unsolved murder aside, and he was sure he'd be able to wrap this one up today if he could get his head straight. But, what the hell was going on today? It wasn't just this bug; people were behaving very peculiarly.

The first to arrive had been an older couple. Everything

seemed fine at the start, but as soon as they got inside the house, Steven knew it was a waste of time. They looked sick at the sight of the entrance hallway itself - yes it was all very modern and arty, perhaps a little too young for them - but give it a chance. He didn't even manage to show them past the first bedroom, and now Steven realised he might have caught this bug off them. Maybe it wasn't the hallway that made them look sick.

Can bugs spread that quickly?

After that couple, a younger pair with a child arrived. Perfect, three out, three in. They seemed to like the place well enough and the child absolutely loved it. She couldn't get enough of the front room and just kept whizzing around in circles like she was trying to take off. She had a crazed smile on her face and after several attempts to calm her down, the parents had to drag her flailing body out of the room while she screamed. By the time she got back to the car, she seemed to have calmed down and Steven was pretty sure she was asleep as they buckled her back into their SUV. They said they'd call back.

Ergh, kids.

There were a couple of normal viewings after that, but then out of nowhere, Steven had fallen ill and puked into the bathroom sink while he was showing a single man the various hands-free features of the modern sink unit. "Here's your soap, water and..." Puke. This apparently set the potential buyer off too, as the smell of puke sometimes does, but the man managed to get outside and control himself.

Then, following a short rest, he received a very excited looking couple, and thought they were the ones. They asked all the right questions and smiled ear to ear.

He waited in the garden after giving them some space to look around, but when he re-entered the house, they'd gone. He rarely got dine-and-dashers, and they hadn't looked the type - he certainly wouldn't have left them alone if that had been the case. He thought about phoning them to make sure they were ok, but then felt that special kind of slippery saliva building in his mouth getting ready to pave the way for what was left of his breakfast. That's when he'd fertilised the flowers. That was it so far. Five down, one interested and the rest crazy.

The market had slowed over winter, which was pretty standard stuff, but Steven had a few more bits on finance than he would have liked, on account of a successful summer. He needed this sale more than he'd like to admit. He took another swig from the bottle; his stomach seemed to allow this. His eyes wandered around the outline of the house, taking in its features. Nice old stock brickwork, grand design vibes, quiet street and chain free.

Yeah, tidy. Come on Stevie, get your shit together.

The current owners had vacated the night of the crime. Apparently, their daughter couldn't stand being in the house anymore and refused to sleep there another night, or so they had said. It was Steven who had picked up the phone in the office when they called. As they were now staying in Devon, all liaison with Mr. and Mrs. Howard had been done over the phone. He went over the call once more in his head.

"Well it's probably about time we upsized anyway," Mr. Howard had said. "It's a... shame. We put a lot of work into that house as you can see. It was quite the project. But it's an odd building, quite impractical. Ivy could do with a bigger room, she's growing up now. And I wouldn't mind more home office space. Somewhere a bit quieter."

Steven read between the lines and knew Mr. Howard really meant he wanted a house where dead men wouldn't be greeting them when they arrive home from their weekly shop. Unfortunately, estate agents can't guarantee that as part of the package, but it left a house to be sold and Steven wasn't going to turn them down, even with the house's chequered past. It was a belter. Mr. Howard was open to offers, in a rush to sell, and had agreed to some borderline immoral selling rates from the office. He had finished by telling Steven they wouldn't be returning until the sale had gone through. Steven's thoughts were interrupted by the hum of a vehicle approaching. He prayed they wouldn't be time wasters. He watched as two women exited a small hatchback and approached. They looked like sisters.

Going halfsies maybe?

Feeling better, he waved and gave them his best welcome.

'Hi, I'm Mona. I spoke with Steven?'

'Hiya. Yup, that's me.' He reached into the car, took a brochure off the dash and shut the door, hoping to leave his sickness in there to suffocate. 'Have you come far?'

'No, I'm local. Hoping this might be the one. What do you think, sis?' She chuckled a little and looked at the other woman who was staring at the house. After a gentle shoulder nudge she managed a light smile, then went to introduce herself.

'Hi, I'm Rachel.'

'Nice to meet you both. Shall we?' He led on with his hand, and they made their way up the path until he remembered the sick. 'Oh, actually. It's best we take the driveway. The footpath is a little slippery. I nearly went over myself this morning.'

They both looked in the general direction of the sick but he was sure they wouldn't be able to pick it out. As they hit the driveway, he began to feel a little nauseous again. Each step he took seemed to rattle his teeth and he felt his temperature rising once again, like he was getting closer to some kind of bonfire. By the time they'd made it to the top of the drive, his legs were like jelly and he unbuttoned his shirt further, hearing Mr. Baumann tut loudly in his head.

'Door's open,' he said, breathlessly. 'Head on in.' He saw Mona pause briefly at the front door to look back at her sister. She looked a bit uncertain of something.

Mona opened up the front door and let her sister pass, holding the door open for Steven. He pushed himself to make up the distance. He had to get this thing sold, and she had sounded very interested on the phone. He squeezed a thank you out of his lungs as he passed Mona. Rachel stood in the hallway and smiled at him in a very odd manner, almost as if the rest of her face was unaware of the fact.

What's with all these weirdos today?

Maybe he was hallucinating with fever. His ears pounded as if he were a thousand leagues under the sea. Steven took a few more steps inside the house, then felt heat rise rapidly through his foot, wrap around his spine and engulf his brain.

As the floor came up to meet his descending face, Steven had the strangest feeling it might be the house making him sick, but then it all went black.

26

'Bloody idiots, both of them,' Teddy said, as he tossed a rock into the sea. He had been chewing on last night's meeting with Adrian and Caz, and no matter what side he chewed on, it left a bitter taste in his mouth. He rubbed his left shoulder with his free hand. He sometimes forgot how old his body was despite his mind ticking away like a well-oiled machine. He eyed up a pebble that had broken away from the stony beach and lay stranded on the short stretch of sand before the shoreline. He empathised with it. Clearly, it belonged on one side of the beach, yet it had allowed itself to be pulled from its home, hypnotised by the mysteries of the deep sea as it slid its tendrils around it, whispering gifts of greener pastures. He was just like that miserable pebble. Dropped into no man's land in another universe, in the same bloody town, but not the one that the brochure offered; where lovers smiled handsomely with Nobel Laureate medals bouncing off their chests as they walked down the promenade. Teddy clenched both fists and kicked the stone into the sea.

'Bloody idiot!' he shouted at the top of his voice. He instantly felt self-conscious at his little outburst and looked around the beach. A man looked at him from the other side of the wooden groynes, smartly dressed with his hands deep in his knee-length overcoat. Oddly, he didn't look away as you would expect from the shrinking violets that were the British. Instead, he just stared at Teddy. Teddy wasn't quite sure when this man had shown up, or if he'd been watching him this whole time, but he immediately felt uneasy. He pondered leaving the beach, but that felt like a guilty action and he wasn't actually doing anything wrong. Instead, he turned back out to sea, closed his eyes and drew a deep breath.

He calmed down and let his senses tingle. His nose picked up the salty air and his ears filled with the lapping of the waves. Waves, he thought. The very thing that got this bus rolling. It was not so long ago, in a universe not so far away, that Teddy stood on this very beach and it had all clicked into place. The waves ebbing and flowing in front of him, mirroring the waves that ebbed and flowed over countless scientific papers in the world of physics. It was as if the waves had lifted him up like that very stone, gently carrying him along in that chain of thought and bringing him to rest at the edge of the universe, where his brain waves had been trying to direct him all along. It was the solution to unlocking a bridge: the waves of the Cosmic Microwave Background. The echo of the universe. In order to open a door, you just had to get the key to shout at the lock. Show the lock that there was more than one key.

Back in his world Teddy had rigged a myriad of old televisions together, the show of choice - static. Static that was calling out to other universes thanks to some tinkering from Teddy and some added power from the generator. It wasn't only the power that had done it. The generator still held a dormant line to the grid, its latticework stretching all over the town working as a giant antenna. It was perfect. And it had all become clear when Adrian had jokingly suggested that they simply step through the screen into another world. The practical side wasn't so different - they just needed a signal. Now, he stood on the other side of the door.

This calmed him further, once again drilling into his head the tremendous feat he had managed to achieve. Sure, this world was not as identical as he would have hoped, but he was starting to think he may have meant to arrive in this world, without Adrian, just to find him again. The universe certainly did work in mysterious ways. Teddy was beginning to think it was quite the romantic. Or it had a sick sense of humour.

He nodded at this and brought himself back to the present. Once again, the sea had allowed him to clear his head. It really did blow away the cobwebs. Teddy began making his way back up the beach. He glanced at the man on the other side of the groynes, but he now stood looking out to the sea. The sun had just started setting, throwing out long wavelength reds against the sky.

Waves.

There was that word again. Teddy smiled as he walked into the town.

So the meeting hadn't exactly gone as he'd hypothesised. He had spilled the beans earlier than planned, but was it all that bad? At least now, they could mull it over. Even though he hadn't had the chance to properly explain it, they had a big reason to want to believe him. It explained the other Adrian.

The fact they hadn't gone to the police already was bizarre. But then again, what would someone do if one moment they lost a partner, and the next, said partner alive and well? Teddy didn't have to think hard to put himself in that boat. He'd just lost his Adrian, and yet another lived. Sure, the Adrian in this world was different, but you couldn't get much closer. Teddy knew *this* Adrian would be better off without that feral woman just as the other Adrian was in Teddy's world. She was holding him back, steering him off course, making him play house when he could be with Teddy. He could once again expand his mind. Learn the mysteries of the cosmos and actually travel them now.

Teddy needed Adrian back at his side if he was to continue his work and see other worlds: that was imperative. They had been fairly sure they were travelling into an almost identical world, but calculations could only go so far. Contingencies were made where possible, but he'd been completely knocked for six when he had to deal with not only the loss of Adrian, but an alternative reality to the one he'd come from. The canvas was the same, the paints, the colours, but the brush strokes had little nuisances he hadn't accounted for. A forgery. But, who could determine which was the original? Teddy and Adrian had both known there was potential for a completely different world out there. It could have been covered in ice, scorched with lava, or even flooded, but they both knew what they were doing was far more important, and frankly, downright exciting.

Teddy fantasised about actually picking up a Nobel

Prize for his work, but comically, the only way to show it worked would be to step through another bridge and most likely never return. Jumping from universe to universe, messing the inhabitants around, would certainly cause a stir. Perhaps he'd get caught by some cosmic police force that would lock him up for letting the cat out the bag. Once again, he'd floated off and came back to his senses just as he arrived outside his new residence. A hostel - smaller and cheaper. He stood outside filling his lungs one last time.

'What are you going to do when you get in there?' he said to himself.

Roll up into a ball and cry.

'No. You're going to get your shit together and get a plan in place.'

Can't we just cry some more?

'No more crying.'

I miss Adrian.

'I know. But soon, he'll be ours.'

Soon.

27

Adrian sat with his head in hands. He was looking at his two knights lying a square away from each other on the chessboard in front of him. He'd stupidly allowed an opposing pawn to waltz up to them, which now threatened to take one or the other, and there was nothing he could do about it.

'Would you like a fine stallion, sir?' Adrian said to the empty room. ''Tis the finest in all the land.'

'Well. Don't mind if I do,' he replied to himself in a shrill voice. 'How much?'

'Ah. Well, for you Mr. Computer, nothing! Nothing at all. My ignorance will pay the price.'

Adrian prepared himself for the slaughter that would no doubt happen on the computer's next move. He hadn't protected his pieces and he had to foot the bill. It was a good lesson, but unfortunately, he kept repeating the same mistake. Much like his dances to satisfy his obsessions, he kept repeating the same moves in chess. What was that quote about repetition and insanity, he thought? No doubt he qualified.

The self-imposed house arrest had Adrian working overtime in the cleanliness and order department, each compulsion taking longer than it had the day before. Rearranging the downstairs cupboards had revealed this old, but seldom used, digital chess board sandwiched between various other board games and forgotten paperwork. Rearranging was still to be done, but he'd managed to jam a spanner in the dance for the time being. He had started playing chess again and was getting into it. As predicted, the computer licked its binary lips and took Adrian's undefended knight. He mirrored this move on the board, removing his knight and sliding the pawn into the hoof marks where the knight had stood.

'Ah, sod it.'

He unfurled himself from the floor and stretched his body which happily clicked as he did so. He let his arms flop down and looked around for his next distraction, burned by the recent loss of his knight. Teddy's satchel caught his eye and he felt a pang of guilt.

Caz and Adrian still hadn't told Mona about Teddy. They didn't want to drag her in any deeper than she needed to, in case this went South.

In case it went South? We're off the fucking map matey.

Adrian had only skimmed through the documents Teddy had left. Caz hadn't even entertained the idea. The explanation Teddy had given had refused to settle in. Caz and Adrian were aware of the parallel universe concept in fiction, but in reality, their sense of relief had washed any intrigue away, even on Adrian's behalf. When Teddy told them the other Adrian hadn't been murdered, it was as if an invisible noose had been removed from his neck. Yes, they might be in a sticky situation with the police but he gathered a situation like this didn't necessarily settle into everyday law. He was now more interested in figuring out a way Caz and him could return to normal life. Adrian had even tried to talk Caz out of visiting the house with Mona. As far as he was concerned, that mystery could die a death now they knew the truth and they should focus on putting the yarn they'd been spinning back on a spool. It seemed Caz wanted to keep up appearances with Mona for now, more to protect her then anything else. She had gotten a bit too good at lying since the incident.

Adrian went into the kitchen to make a cup of tea. He peeked around the blinds into the garden as he emptied the kettle, refilled it, swished it around, emptied it and refilled it - rinse and repeat. The spring was still struggling to break through. There was no new growth on the trimmed plants, and the trees were still nothing more than veins of wood stretching into the air against an overcast sky. It all looked so dull. He finally flicked on the kettle and waited, trying to avoid looking out the window again. His hand had naturally made its way up to his head and he played with the scab, unable to help himself. This kept him occupied as the kettle boiled, he timed the brew, swapped teaspoons as he added the oat milk, and dinged his teaspoon five times on the side to finish the ritual.

Pain shot through his skull. Adrian brought his hand into view but already knew what he was going to find. The blood on his finger was a familiar sight, while a little bit of scab wedged under his nail was a bonus.

'Fuck sake. Stop it, Hoarding.' He went to the sink to wash up.

Teddy's satchel lingered in view as Adrian sat on the sofa. He went to drink his tea but cupping the side of the mug told him it was still too hot. The satchel stared at him. Now they knew the truth, it felt like homework. It was as if Adrian had been told that aliens had arrived, and had said, "Oh, that's nice," then continued with his boring life. This should be a landmark moment for the human race, yet neither Adrian, or Caz from what he could tell, really gave a shit about what Teddy had said. Adrian bet he would have burnt through a book about parallel universes last year. He never seemed content with what he had, he was distracted by his increasing dances and he was always trying to live in a snapshot that didn't exist. Now, even parallel universes seemed boring.

Really?

His gut was right. This was the stuff of dreams. Was it really possible to go galavanting from world to world, seeing each of humanity's iterations. Maybe even more than humanities, had said aliens arrived in one life - had it gone well? How many had fallen to apocalyptic events? How many even had humans still on them?

Really?

Adrian stood up and snatched the staring satchel off the floor. He rifled through the contents on his way back to the sofa. He removed a handful of loose A4 sheets and plopped himself back on the sofa. He had no idea where to start. The first couple of pages were a mix of words and equations. There was plenty about the Big Bang Theory and the Cosmic Microwave Background. There were a few pages on Super String Theory, but that was well beyond his understanding.

What had Teddy expected them to learn? Adrian had

read consumer level non-fiction, not textbooks, and certainly not peer reviewed research and articles. He had never even stretched to a New Scientist subscription. Looking at the equations, he barely knew what half the symbols were.

He looked closer and made out some kind of arrow missing half its head. Adrian squinted and believed this to be the notation for a vector. The longer he thought on it, the more confident he felt. However, he knew that knowing the name of something didn't make someone smart. It was the knowledge of what the thing did, how to use it effectively and understanding why it existed in the first place. That was the clever bit. Did he know what a vector did? No. No he did not.

He skimmed through a few more pages. The words became sloppier and eventually gave way to more equations and some graphs. He rotated the pages in his hands fruitlessly, not knowing what to make of these either. Soon, the writing stopped completely, and instead there were excited scribbles at the side of more and more complex graphs.

Then came what Adrian could only describe as drawings. Not artistic feats, but something about them did carry an air of beauty. There were symmetrical patterns, waves made in both simple lines and woven strands, random triangles and circles. Some of the waves ran parallel creating a sort of train track. The tracks continued over the page, the patterns randomly shifting but always symmetrical with those on the other side of the track. Then they became truly random, the symmetrical element gone. The waves that had been peaking and troughing in unison had gone out of phase, all dotted with more sporadic bouts of words he could no longer read. Adrian felt his temperature rise a little. The symbols didn't make sense, but he thought he might be getting a better look into Teddy's mind, and he didn't like what he saw. Were these just the random squiggles of a slightly unhinged man? He'd seemed nice enough, considering the circumstances, but he had also seemed fairly...

'What's the word?' Adrian whispered to himself.

It was the unknown. The uncertainty of his motives. Teddy had appeared from thin air, but he had helped clear up a couple of things, even if Adrian and Caz didn't fully buy the story. Adrian shuffled to the last few pages to see where this graphite train track led. The patterns now cut across the page from top to bottom, or was it left to right? He rotated the pages again and viewed the last symbols which might as well have been hieroglyphs at this point. The pages contained two sets of waves that collided just before they peaked. Teddy had made no notes around these, but the space in between them – the elliptical circle that had been created by the lines... it caught his attention. He went to touch them but something inside him pulled his muscles tight, leaving his right index finger hovering an inch above the page. He pulled back his hand and rubbed his thumb and fingertip together, not quite sure what was going on.

'Fuck.'

Adrian realised they had been far too hasty with Teddy. They'd been spurred on by his throbbing head and Caz's threatening attitude. He looked at that last page once more and flipped it over. There was nothing on the other side and the next sheet brought him back to Teddy's initial text-heavy pages. The elliptical voids drew his attention once again. Why did he want to touch them so badly? It almost made sense to him, he could see something beautiful for the briefest moment. Then it was gone.

'This is ridiculous.' He shook the tension out of his right hand, raised his index finger once again and put it onto the paper before his muscles could pull the handbrake again. Nothing happened.

Of course nothing happened, Dumbo.

But something was niggling. Something was familiar. Was he really some science whizz in another world? Was the knowledge there but he needed to tap into it? Was Teddy that tap? The thought caught him off guard, as if he had cheated on Caz. He continued to flick through the pages, excitement bubbling inside all of a sudden. Then his gut wrenched. He'd deciphered something. But it wasn't the equations.

The hurried notes, the mix of graphs. There were two hands at work here. Were these Adrian's notes as well?

That's my handwriting.

He tossed the notes aside and grabbed a pen and pad he'd been using for chess, quickly scribbling down some random notes that had stuck in his head; CMB, phasing, waves, infinite, collapsing bridges. He pulled the notes back and started to compare.

'My god.'

It *was* his handwriting.

Adrian struggled to fight off a terrible shiver that surged through his entire body.

Had Adrian been in denial about the whole thing, why did it all suddenly feel so real, could he also travel across universes…With Teddy?

The familiar rumble of a car pulling into the drive

snapped his attention back. Adrian quickly put away the sheets, not wanting to talk about this with Caz. His heart hammered as he jogged to the door and slid the dead bolts which could only be operated from the inside - the neighbours would start asking questions if Caz had to knock on her own door. Adrian returned to the front room and tried to look calm himself. Shortly after, Caz entered the room. Adrian was blowing on his tea trying to behave naturally. A happy side effect of those new locks was the extra time he got whenever Caz returned home. He wasn't going to get caught doing anything in this house he shouldn't be doing any time soon.

28

Bola had lived in Furlong for over a year now and he'd never gone *into* the South Downs for a walk. He wasn't unfit, he took pride in his health - ok, his physique - but countryside rambling had never really appealed to him. He preferred the coast. There, the sound of the waves soothed any troubles he had and there was always a bubble of activity nearby. The countryside could be barren, lonely.

He would spend hours simply looking out to sea mulling his thoughts or walking along the sandy shoreline when the tide went out. Right now however, his feet were carrying him up a narrow path that wound from the very edge of Furlong's suburbs into the South Downs. To his right, a barren field rose up and away meeting the overcast sky. His left fell off down into a treeline that was dense with ivy, blocking the view of the hillside below.

He'd only been walking for five minutes but Furlong seemed miles behind him already as the vast countryside closed its arms around him. The hum of the A-road gave way to rustling leaves and singing birds while the air lost its sea breeze and took on a damp quality, although still oddly refreshing. Maybe there was something in this rambling after all, Bola thought. Or was that just the butterflies talking?

The night he'd spent with Mona had gone rather well, the morning well again, and it now appeared the attraction might be more than physical. This would be their first official date. Bola had already gone too far in taking Mona home that night, straight after explicitly telling Kim there was nothing to worry about. As he saw it the damage was done. What's a secret rendezvous thrown onto the fire, or indeed something more later on.

More, really?

Maybe.

The one professionalism that remained was in their communication, or lack of. They hadn't exchanged numbers - overkill as Bola saw it, but it seemed to settle Mona. They had done it old school: a time and place.

Mona also had her own concerns about their relationship.

Relationship, really?

Maybe.

From their conversations between the physical actions, it was clear that Caz meant a lot to Mona. Mona sticking herself in the middle of an investigation as to the death of her brother-in-law was strictly a no-no. Caz wasn't just a sister; she was her protector, her captain, her champion. She spoke of Caz with an air of admiration that bordered on childishness. Perhaps that is what their roles really were now, parent and child. Bola was aware of their family situation due to the investigation, but he hadn't broached this with Mona.

That was far too deep for the depths of their current relationship.

There you go again, calling it a relationship.

'Well what else is it?' he mumbled to himself.

Dating. You're just dating. Alright? Although...there is a case that needs solving. Perhaps if you asked Mona–

Nope, nope, nope.

He wasn't planning to use Mona in that way - it would be unlawful as well as darn right immoral.

His belly did a little flip and brought his attention back. He'd just seen a fork in the path, exactly as Mona had described; one fenced with a metal gate, the other a wooden stile - he'd be taking the stile. He popped himself over the top doing his best to keep his jeans clean. What was wrong with a simple gate? He composed himself on the other side and looked down at his trainers, they were covered in mud. He wasn't prepared for this. He tried to scrape off the worst on the stile then headed off down the path again in search of the bench where they'd be meeting.

The treeline fell away and Bola was blessed with a charming view across a valley that he had no idea existed. Below, a flock of sheep peppered the field like fallen clouds. Up on the other side of the valley was a collection of houses. Bola walked on while he let his internal compass calibrate and realised that it must be Cable's Wood. Just as he tried to make out whether he could see Marsh Avenue from here he was interrupted.

'Hey.'

Bola turned his attention back up the path and saw Mona sitting on a bench. Her hair was neatly tucked in a bun allowing her understated beauty to shine. She wore leggings that tucked neatly into muddy walking boots and a bright red windbreaker that hugged her body tightly. He wasn't aware of this previously, but apparently walking gear did it for him. Or was it just Mona? On each occasion they had met Bola did always find himself on the back foot. As if she was exactly where she needed to be, and Bola just happened to chance upon her beauty.

'Hey,' he replied.

'Found me ok then? I wasn't sure how clear I'd been the other morning. I'm glad you came.' She popped up from her seat and headed over to Bola. His stomach started spinning and when she delicately planted a single kiss on his lips he found himself breathless.

Come on man, get a grip.

'Well. Me too,' he said, trying to keep his smile level. He immediately panicked at the sober situation he found himself in and spat the next thing out that came into his head. 'Is that Cable's Wood?'

'Oh,' she said, her smiling fading. 'Yes, it is. I didn't really think about that when I picked this spot.'

Nice one, Bola. Is that where your sister's husband was found dead?

'Sorry. I didn't mean… I wasn't really sure. I've never been to the South Downs.'

'What?' Mona said, snapping back to herself. 'You've never been up the Downs?'

'Up the Downs? That's a bit of an odd saying.'

'Ha, I guess it is. We've always said that though. Since we were kids here. But really? You've been here a year now.'

'Yeah, over a year. I'm just not really a countryside person.'

'Well, that's true,' Mona said, now taking in his attire.

'I like the coast. I just never got this,' he said, looking around. 'Where do you get a coffee? There's coffee all along the seafront.'

'You bring your own up here.'

'Sounds like an effort.'

'Don't worry, I'll get you up to speed. Come on.' With that they set off down the path leaving the mysteries of Cable's Wood across the valley.

29

Adrian was hunched over Caz's mobile phone watching the doorbell's video stream of Teddy standing outside their house. He had returned.

'Well,' Caz said. 'He said he'd be back.'

'A man of his word?'

'It's a bit early to say that. How's he going to explain this nonsense?'

'Is it nonsense though?' Adrian had pored over the articles further, this was no joke.

Caz looked back at him, her eyes soft, 'I don't like that man, I know that much. But I can't deny it seems to be the only explanation that makes sense.'

The buzzer went again.

'Hello?' Teddy's voice carried through the speakers. 'Caz, it's me Teddy.'

'Well, at least he's keeping up the facade for the street, right?' said Adrian. Caz rolled her eyes and made her way to the door.

Teddy tried to say hello but Caz cut him off. 'Yes, yes.

Get in.' She shut the door behind him. 'In case you're wondering, I've already got my tools on me.' Caz landed this blow just as Teddy locked eyes with Adrian, who noticed a slight twitch of panic in Teddy's face. Clearly, he was still getting over the last near miss.

'Hello, Adrian,' Teddy said.

Adrian nodded. 'Tea again?'

Teddy looked at Caz like a dog waiting to be released.

'Go on,' she said, nodding Teddy onwards. 'No drawn out stories again please. Pick up where you left off and cut the crap,' she said in complete honesty.

Blimey, Adrian thought.

She's been waiting for this.

Perhaps Caz had been more desperate to see Teddy again than she'd let on.

'Well, I'm glad you said that,' Teddy replied, walking through. 'I've been going over our last meeting and it became clear to me that, yes, I may have gone about things in the wrong way. Perhaps I should have been more direct. You're both adults. You should be able to hear the truth.' Teddy walked over to what was becoming his regular seat. 'Grasping it is a different matter, and you'll just have to get there in your own time.'

Adrian prepared drinks and handed them out.

'Thank you. Did you have a chance to look over the paperwork I left?' Teddy asked.

'Yes,' Adrian answered for both of them.

'And did it make sense?' Teddy asked.

'No,' Adrian said.

Teddy did not seem surprised at this. 'No,' Teddy repeated, dully. 'And why would it? You both completely jumped the gun and forced me to tell you what happened in the crudest possible way.'

Adrian was a bit perplexed. He felt like he was being told off by a teacher. He went to defend himself but Caz was several steps ahead of him.

'Excuse me? You were the one who left without explaining anything. You were the one who–'

'Yet, you didn't stop me,' Teddy interrupted. 'I don't know why you didn't, but I seized the opportunity nonetheless and it allowed me to think. I apologise. Truly. Thankfully, both your minds didn't explode with the information. I did worry that the universe might have slipped some kind of kill-switch into every sentient being's head, should they ever discover the secrets it wove into the fabric of existence nearly fourteen billion years ago. We need not worry. As such,' Teddy reached into his pocket and pulled out a mobile phone, 'I thought I'd show it to you rather than explain it this time. It's only a short video, but it'll save time, and a bit of visual learning always helps things stick.'

Adrian got the meaning of his sentence but let it slide. Admittedly, he was already enticed by a video explanation.

'And if it's fake?' Caz said.

Teddy appeared not to hear her. 'Here, take it. I had a bit of a job recovering the data, but it's all there. Fascinating really.'

Adrian took the phone from Teddy, positioning it so that he and Caz could both see it. As his eyes came to rest on the screen, he saw the static image of a man asleep on a bed, a floating play button sitting on his chest like a giant digital medallion. Adrian thought the sleeping man looked familiar and brought the screen a little closer. He did know the man waiting to perform in the video. He knew him very well indeed.

Of course, it's bloody me.

He hadn't known what to expect but it certainly brought on a truck load of the creeps looking at another version of himself.

Most people never know when they're going to die. Some may know how they're going to die, but not when. But, with absolute certainty, Adrian was sure he was the only person in the world – this world at least – who would get to watch a video answering both of those questions in glorious high definition.

30

'Adrian! Adrian! Wake up! It's beautiful! It's absolutely beautiful!' Teddy said, shaking him awake.

'Christ, Teddy. What?' Adrian said. He was disorientated and struggling to place himself, he then remembered he was on Teddy's bed - a mattress pushed to the side of the room - in the generator building he was a live-in guardian of. 'What time is it? What are you smiling about? You look like a mad man.'

He really did, and he was afraid of what it meant. He had the most grotesque smile on his face. It made Adrian feel uneasy. It didn't fit the ecstatic mood he was in. Teddy was prone to fits of mania, but this seemed different. Worse.

'Pah!' Teddy clapped him on the shoulder and shoved his phone in Adrian's face, the torch almost blinding him. 'Nothing, my good man, will be *mad* after this. Are you ready, my darling?'

Teddy was towering over Adrian, blocking the view to the rest of the room. He could see Teddy's pulse thumping in his throat. Had they really done it? Or was this just another false alarm? Adrian wasn't entirely sure of all the intricacies of the process – that was Teddy's job – but he knew they were close. Had Teddy's carefully curated signal, which called out through the ether, grabbed onto a corresponding wave to complete the connection? Something had been stirring for days now, something was yawning, as if slowly awakening and shrugging off the dust. Bridges that were once perhaps frequently used but had long since seized

'A world is listening Adrian,' Teddy said.

Adrian's skin crawled.

'It is?'

Adrian felt an odd wave of euphoria building. Was Teddy's excitement rubbing off on him?

No.

An energy stirred behind Teddy, it enveloped Adrian and Teddy's enthusiasm now made sense. He felt a twitch in his mouth, and an uncontrollable smile made its way up to his ears. His heart beat harder, pushing the essence of his life around his body faster, feeding his organs, his muscles, his soul. He knew something had happened, and there was only one thing for it. Teddy brought Adrian to his feet then stepped aside.

Adrian staggered at the presence of something he couldn't fathom. It was incomparable to anything he had ever felt, seen, heard or read. He gawped at the wall of televisions where some unknown energy emanated in waves and swaddled him. He felt as if he was in the bosom of the cosmos – a place of infinite energy, density, chaos and purpose. He wanted to run head first and dive right into it, but his knees buckled as if the energy demanded his fealty first, to bow at the feet of eternity. He collapsed down, feeling as though his body was no longer his.

What had they done?

Teddy was shortly kneeling at his side, his once delicate frame now invigorated with energy from the lapping waves of the cosmos.

'It's beautiful, isn't it?' Teddy said. Adrian had no words. He tried to look away, to give his mind time to think. In the corner of his eye he saw that their bags had been pulled into the room. Prepared long ago for a trip that Adrian honestly didn't think would ever come. But, here he saw the time had come, and Teddy's preparation had been justified. Teddy thrust the mobile into Adrian's hands.

'Adrian. Take it. We must document this.'

'I...' His mouth was dry. He tried to swallow.

Phone? Document?

He didn't even know if he could control his arms. It felt unimportant.

'Adrian, we must,' Teddy said. 'It will be the only way to show people.'

'Yes, but...' Adrian struggled again. 'It's beautiful. We did this? This?' As the words left his mouth, he felt his smile widen, almost as if it were answering his own question. Teddy grabbed his chin with a free hand and planted the most extraordinary kiss onto his mouth. It surged through him. He wanted him. Now.

'Too late for that,' Teddy said, as if he'd read his thoughts. 'Yes.' Adrian nodded. He took the phone and framed up Teddy. Teddy took a breath then began.

'Ladies and gentleman. Peers, colleagues, doubters.

Today is the first day of... of the rest of eternity,' Teddy said into the camera.

Eternity?

Did Adrian tell him to say that? It was eerily fitting, as if he would have used the same words.

'For before us,' Teddy continued, 'lies a gateway to other worlds. I hypothesise this world is just like ours. A blue planet. Teeming with life. Not with aliens but with humans, animals, invertebrates. Filled with other mes and other yous. Other Elton Johns. Other Dalia Lamas.'

Adrian smiled even wider. Had Teddy rehearsed this?

'It is almost identical to ours, because it exists here, now, parallel to us, as I'm sure many others do, hidden behind a veil fabricated by the cosmos. A veil that we have lifted.' Teddy extended his arm as a master of ceremonies might introduce the next act. Adrian took the cue and looked to the televisions where the source of the energy was coming from. But there was nothing to visually confirm its presence. Just a wall of static.

Glorious static.

Adrian panned the phone around to get the televisions in shot, looking down at the screen to check the framing.

Adrian's heart palpitated wildly.

He went to call Teddy, but whatever moisture he had managed to get back into his mouth had once again evaporated. His mouth lay open catching flies. Adrian struggled to make sense of what he was seeing on the screen. He looked back at the wall of televisions with his own eyes, pinpointing the energy easily, but there was nothing to see. He looked back at the phone, almost afraid to do so, in case it was still there: it was.

A catastrophe of colour was pulsing in and out of

existence from a tear in what he could only imagine was the fabric of spacetime. Its light whipped into the room like solar filaments. This isn't science, Adrian thought. This is magic. Terrifying magic. Adrian watched the filaments reach out further, extinguishing themselves as they went.

'And now, my devoted audience,' Teddy continued, kicking Adrian rather hard in the side to get his attention. Anger flashed through Adrian in a heartbeat. He'd never felt anger so visceral.

I'll rip his fucking head off if he does that again.

As quick as it had come, the anger went, but it had felt very real. Adrian apologised out loud for his thoughts, but Teddy didn't seem to hear, so enveloped he was in his monologue.

'We bid you farewell as we make our journey onwards.' Teddy stood and grabbed the bags from the corner of the room and passed Adrian his own. Adrian hoisted the bag onto his back while keeping the phone pointed in the same direction, then rose to his feet. He made his way forward, invigorated.

'Let's do this!' Adrian cheered.

Stop!

Adrian managed to compose himself and step back from what was happening. It was madness. There was no way he was stepping through that door, no fucking way in hell. *Hell* might even be on the other side. He didn't want to die in the heart of the sun or whatever that thing was. He had a life, a good life. He had friends, family, reasons to live. He had Teddy. He'd retrained in an area he was passionate about, and he enjoyed working with Teddy. He *loved* Teddy. He felt the uncontrollable smile twitch on his face again. It was pulling him into the energy, like he had been caught on the hook of some cosmic rod. He took another step towards it.

No.

'Yes!'

Adrian gulped hard and let the euphoria swaddle him once again. He was ready to dive, to die. He progressed forward, ready to break into a sprint. Something was telling him to actually *jump* into the bridge. He bounded forward but a few steps in a wave of energy blasted over him. Adrian lost his balance and hit the floor. Teddy held his ground.

Something has changed...

Adrian's doubt returned. He tried to push it away and reboot the feelings he had a moment ago, when he knew this was the path he must take. But now, something more than the combined power of his mind, body and soul was telling him to stay back, far back. It was telling him to run. He listened and took a few more steps back, the enthusiasm in his cinematography failing. He let the phone drop to his side, filming nothing but the wall. He even felt the smile fall from his face, punching him in the stomach as it went, leaving a nauseating feeling.

'Teddy, are you sure? I don't feel right, something has changed. I don't think we're meant to go through.' His belly rumbled and he swallowed down some vomit that was threatening to escape.

'Adrian, look at me.' Teddy was suddenly at his side, the hideous grin still plastered on his face. 'This is our purpose.' He seemed unchanged, still euphoric, and in Adrian's new frame of mind, still crazy. Adrian's insides were bubbling as if he'd consumed a large amount of squid that had suddenly decided to reanimate inside him. Vomit once again scuttled up his throat and made it into his mouth. The acid burned his gums. He knew he should be excited, but his temperature was rising and his vision was blurring. He tried to blink it away, taking further steps back until he met resistance. Teddy was blocking his path.

That smile, that terrifying smile.

It didn't even fit Teddy's face anymore. Adrian saw it so clearly now. It belonged to some deranged being, not of this world or any other, to something that lurked in between the dimensions of reality like a parasite waiting for a host. Teddy's eyes were vacant. Adrian felt weaker by the second. He went to shrug Teddy off, but he might as well have been boxing in his sleep.

'Adrian, let us go into eternity,' Teddy said. 'Together.' Teddy clasped both of Adrian's hands and pinned the phone between them. He walked Adrian back towards the energy. Adrian's feet followed for the first few steps, keeping him upright, but then they buckled as if some safety mechanism had kicked in. He felt himself falling backwards, waiting for the thud of the floor to bring him out of this nightmare. A nightmare filled with the gruesome smile of eternity.

31

Teddy had watched the video carefully over the past few days. He was aware Adrian had lost the will to film and the end was rather messy - Adrian had been feeling a last minute *push* from the universe - but Teddy had edited and purposefully distorted the final minutes. They would never know. He asked them to watch those final moments again. They watched silently, and after they had finished the third watch, Teddy decided it was time to continue.

'I'm still not entirely sure what happened – why *I* survived and Adrian did not. It was likely our combined ignorance of the unknown that killed him.'

Adrian and Caz looked up at Teddy, confused.

Teddy began his lies. 'Adrian was not meant to travel over the bridge that night, but our free will allowed us to. I now know why.'

Teddy waited for the tell-tale signs of someone who couldn't resist the carrot that had been dangled over their own head. People simply like to know things, and neither Adrian nor Caz disappointed.

'You're telling me you used TVs to jump across universes?' Caz said.

'It's a little more complicated than that. But they are a suitable tool for the job. They are able to detect part of the Cosmic Microwave Background through their antennae, echos of the Big Bang. It's the edge of what we can document as the wavelengths travel so far. Adrian, the *other* Adrian, theorised that if it was a sort of "edge" perhaps we could peek beyond it. And on the other side you would find–'

'Us,' Adrian finished.

'Precisely. The generator building that I was a live-in guardian for served as a gigantic antenna with its lattice work of underground cables. It made for the signal we could afford - we didn't have donors falling over each other to help us.'

Idiots. Now who's crazy?

'We made a signal that could bring other universes into a clearer view. But what finally happened when the connection was made, that is unknown. That's the beauty of science: sometimes we don't know why things behave in the way they do. That's what drives us forward. We were certain we could make a connection, how to pass through had always been the larger question. I now know that the bridge is constantly changing. There may be a way to stabilise it, fix it to one reality. But your feelings, I believe they're linked to three distinct types of reality. I have been going back to Marsh Avenue to try and quantify the effects of the bridge on us humans.' A shiver ran through his body as his mind raced ahead of his words. These weren't lies. These were the magnificent workings of the cosmos.

'I think I've felt it.' Surprisingly, it was Caz who spoke up. 'Something happened to Adrian too that night.'

'Good. That's all part of the mechanics. Let me explain.'

For the first time, Caz seemed genuinely interested in what Teddy had to say. This was finally going to plan. He hoped that Adrian had taken time to look at the curated notes and find his own handwriting in the pages - would he start to stray?

Teddy composed himself and continued.

'In the first instance, you can cross. I even believe something *wants* you to cross and it is safe to do so. The feeling was...' Teddy had to stop. His left leg jiggled like that of an excited child. He had to be careful. Teddy had to do this right and win their trust. He couldn't lose *this* Adrian too. 'I apologise. The trip takes quite an emotional toll,' he said in his most academic tone. Teddy laboriously went to take a sip of his tea, hoping one of them would say something.

'I think I've felt that one,' Adrian said.

Teddy quickly swallowed his mouthful of tea. 'On the night it happened?'

'No. The night we snuck in, when it was raining. When we saw you. I had my hand on the door handle and–'

'You felt the pull.' Teddy let his words hang in the room, hoping Adrian would feel some symbolic connection in the feelings they had each felt.

'I felt the opposite. It wasn't a pull,' Caz said.

'Well, every time is different, even for me,' Teddy said. 'In the past few days, I've felt push and pull, each in varying degrees of intensity. Sometimes it's barely a whisper. I had to go right up to the front door once to see if

I could feel it. Other times, I could feel it easily. Now I know the feeling, it's like I can tune into it, almost like reading music, but you have to know how. It's a dangerous language to learn, so I won't go into it.' Another lie. 'In addition to this, there are times when there is nothing at all – no push, no pull. No matter how close I was, or how hard I tried to read the feelings again. In those instances, I believe the bridge to be shut, for me at least. Perhaps it's still active for other potential travellers. What I now hypothesise is that the intensity has a direct correlation to the similarities of the parallel world. The stronger it is, the more similar I believe the other world to be. The most important factor for all of us is that the connection is still active, the bridge is still turning through worlds. It continues to be powered from my world. In fact, I'm sure of it now.'

'How sure?' Adrian asked. Teddy had to keep his composure. Was Adrian interested in a trip perhaps?

'Go on,' Caz said, teasing him. It was clear she knew exactly where Teddy's buttons were and he was concerned that if she kept pushing, she would figure out what each button did, and then his true motives would come to light.

'I hypothesise, based on my experience and research, that that is the case. For both the power and rotation.' Teddy's anger that Adrian had coupled up with this woman once again boiled.

What on earth did he see in her? He'd be so much happier without her, can't he see that?

'So, what was Caz feeling?' Adrian asked, clearly trying to smooth over the tension.

'Well, if Caz wasn't feeling the pull, she was most likely feeling the push. The second type of reality. Where another you – most likely an identical you when it comes to a molecular level – exists on the other side of the bridge. The universes didn't want her to cross. It's not safe, so it simply lets you know.'

'And the feelings – or the bridge – rotates in some way?' Adrian said.

'Yes, in a way,' Teddy said.

'Are you able to track the cycles?' Adrian asked.

'Ha. That's a good question, but unfortunately, it appears to be random.' Teddy lied again. He had already begun tracking cycles and believed he knew the formula. 'It simply invites or warns.'

'Like it tried to warn your Adrian?' Caz asked.

'Caz.' Adrian placed a hand on her thigh. Teddy's anger simmered at the sight of Adrian's hand, not Caz's stab.

'Yes,' Teddy said coolly while looking into her eyes. 'And we didn't listen. I didn't listen. We'd been trying for so long to cross… And now I have to live with that. But I won't let it happen again now I know the dangers. If you're not meant to cross, you shouldn't cross. That much is very clear to me now. I don't know who makes these rules. But, stay put and you're safe.'

'When I went to go and view the house, the agent passed out and bashed his head. That didn't look that safe to me.'

'He's fine,' Teddy said.

'How do you know that?'

'Because I've been keeping an eye on the house and I followed it up. Go ahead, phone the agency.'

'We believe you,' Adrian said.

'Do we?' Caz said, like it was news to her.

'Yes, we do. Because that's what happened to me, the night of the murder,' Teddy winced at this and Adrian caught it. 'Or whatever we're to call it. I threw up everywhere and passed out. I'm still here, aren't I?'

'Did you really?' Teddy asked, fascinated that individuals on the receiving side of a journey also felt the effects.

'Yes, I've never thrown up like that. I thought it was–' Adrian stopped himself, clearly covering something up. Teddy could tell it was more out of embarrassment than skulduggery. The mannerisms or both Adrian's were identical and he knew them well.

'Fascinating. And where were you that night? Clearly you weren't here on account of the police situation you find yourself in?'

'Just *out*.' Adrian was being coy about something and Teddy had to push. This could be valuable information.

'Excuse my prying, but this could all be helpful research.' Adrian and Caz exchanged a glance. Every interaction between the two, every unspoken word, prickled Teddy with anger.

Just talk to me, forget about her.

'I was near thirty-three Marsh Avenue.'

'Incredible,' Teddy said. This *was* useful information. 'How close?'

'Well, actually just down the road. Round the bend going south.'

'Absolutely fascinating.' Teddy mulled this over silently. Even when Adrian wasn't working directly with Teddy, he still brought fresh thoughts and revelations to the table. This was what made Adrian so important. He was the key to Teddy's own Pandora's Box. He needed that key back in his life, whatever it took. Teddy shared his thoughts with the room, feeling he was in class again.

'So, back to the night of the journey. The intensity of the bridge must have exponentially grown in those final moments, so much so it sent a warning shot to you to keep your distance on this side as well. It rendered you useless, incapacitating you to avoid you getting any closer.'

'But, why didn't your Adrian pass out?' Caz enquired.

'I'm not sure,' he lied again, knowing he may well have passed out if Teddy hadn't pushed him through. 'I believe it's because he knew the language already, subconsciously perhaps. He was extraordinary, knowing things without consciously knowing them,' he suggested quickly, although the thought wasn't that outlandish. Caz let it drop, and Adrian picked up where they'd left off.

'Well, the people I was with seemed fine from what I could tell. I was the only one throwing up, and no one was running up the road to thirty-three wanting to jump in. But either way, it passed – very quickly, actually. So that must have been the moment you arrived? Then, I was absolutely fine.'

'Barely. One version of you is dead,' Caz said, clearly annoyed at the conversation Teddy and Adrian were having alone.

'Caz, please,' Adrian said. 'Don't you want to get to the bottom of this?'

'I thought we had. I thought we were done after the last meeting. I frankly don't know what else you want from us, Teddy. You said your piece last time.'

'I want to help you understand.'

'But I don't need to. You even said we don't need to understand this *language* you're on about. I'm not a scientist and I'm certainly not a dimensional traveller or whatever you call yourself.'

'You do need to understand,' Teddy said.

'Why Teddy? Why? Do you need our help?' There she went again, getting ahead of herself. Luckily it was in the right direction. Luckily it was part of his plan.

Luckily.

'You *do* need our help, don't you?' she said.

'I'll get to that,' Teddy replied, playing coy.

Caz surveyed him in silence and Adrian sat dumbly at her side, then she said the very words that might well serve as her own undoing. 'You're stranded here aren't you?'

Teddy let the lie settle, then nodded. 'Yes.'

'Yes,' she repeated. They got there faster than intended. Caz was infuriating yet wickedly smart, but regardless of who was steering this conversation, Teddy was happy with the outcome.

'And I'll need you there to close the bridge, to make sure no one else gets hurt.' It was the crucial lie to get Adrian on site too.

'But, won't that be dangerous?' Adrian asked.

'Very astute concern, Adrian. However, remember the free will and language I spoke about? It's best to think of these pushes and pulls like invitations.' Teddy pointed to the hallway for a practical example. 'Your doorway. You could walk through that now if you wanted, but you are still sitting here. The door is open, it is inviting you to go through, but you still have free will. You are the commander of your response to that invitation. The pull is merely showing you what's for dinner, it is your choice whether you reply. If you understand the language the invitation is written in, the stock of the paper, the font, then you might be in danger. Adrian and myself *wanted* to travel through. We created the bridge and it was our *purpose* to travel through, we were just unaware of the risks. As you could see by the video, we were happy to travel through – me in particular with my shamefully arrogant speech. It's possible Adrian might have felt a push at the last moment, but ignored it. As you can see, we still jumped hand-in-hand.' Teddy wondered if either of them would question this. Teddy knew the full force of the bridge, but he believed he'd spun enough lies to cover its true workings and tremendous lure.

'So, the bridge was protecting me?' Adrian asked. 'It knew another version of me was on the way and kept me put.'

'Yes. The whole street would have been sucked in by now if it was that powerful.'

'I suppose so,' Adrian replied.

Teddy panicked thinking Adrian might see through the lies. He knew the conflict Adrian felt was his latent thinking power trying to break through. He really could not wait to have him back. Even in this infant state of thinking, he was still something to behold. 'Look. I'm the one travelling so you've really nothing to worry about. You can't die in a plane crash if you're still at the airport. I am the one in danger.'

Manipulating Adrian's kindness had been Teddy's plan, but it was Caz who placed the next action on the table. Likely not out of kindness, but determination to see the back of Teddy once and for all. Perhaps he should have relied more on Caz this whole time.

'Show us the bridge, and I'll pack your bags for you,' Caz finished.

'And you'll shut the bridge behind me?'

'Is it complicated?'

'As easy as turning off a TV.'

The final lie.

So, it was settled. Teddy had them onboard as planned. He spent the next few moments briefly going through the plan, fabricating their involvement, which consisted of them coming to 33 Marsh Avenue when he called them. The tension in the room slackened with this course of action. The cards were on the table and everyone seemed happy with the flop, turn and river, but Teddy had played them with a trick deck. There was even a polite goodbye as he left this time, and Caz's tools didn't make another appearance. As Teddy donned his jacket, Adrian asked a final question.

'The third reality, with no push or pull,' Adrian asked. 'What is it?'

Teddy smiled at his star pupil. His Adrian had never left a stone unturned, and it seemed this one wouldn't either. Teddy couldn't wait for them to work together again, to be together again. His appetite had been whetted and Teddy was sure if he managed to get this Adrian to himself, he would become the Adrian he knew and loved. That was his final card trick in this game. Teddy answered the question, which had the gravest of answers.

'Well. There isn't one.'

Teddy zipped his parka up to the top and helped himself to the locks, cracking the door open and letting a stiff breeze shoot through. 'It ceased to be at some point in the past.' And with that, he took his leave.

32

If Bola could tell anyone about the clandestine relationship he was having with Mona, he'd tell them one thing: the sex was great. He watched with a smile as Mona left the room in nothing but her birthday suit. He still wasn't sure if it was the illicit nature of the relationship that was contributing to this, or that they were a good match in bed. One night stands weren't uncommon for Bola, he found they especially happened without much trying in a club. There was less talking, more dancing. He knew deep down he was work obsessed and narcissistic - it didn't make for good flirting or boyfriend material.

At first Bola had been worried that with work conversation off the table - due to the situation they found themselves in - he'd struggle to keep anything going. However, without this to fall back on, he seemed to have produced a reasonable amount of acceptable conversation. He was freed of the shackles that normally made things fizzle away. They'd managed to navigate the waters, that from a distance seemed troubled with obstacles, and were having a genuinely good time together. The walks had become more frequent, as too had the sleepovers.

He got himself out of bed, threw on half his clothes and headed to the kitchen. It was a Saturday and neither of them had work today. He wasn't quite sure if they'd be spending the day together or he'd be taking his leave shortly. He flicked the kettle on just as Mona's buzzer went - she was still in the shower and he had a slight dilemma as to the protocol here. He wasn't meant to be here, whoever it was. He cautiously made his way across the kitchen to the attached lounge to have a peek out the window: there was a supermarket van outside with its orange lights flashing. Trying to be helpful he dashed to the bathroom and tried the door but it was locked.

Clearly she's not that comfortable yet.

'Mona. You've got a delivery,' Bola said, hoping she would be able to hear over the noise of the shower.

'What?'

'Supermarket. Delivery.' He heard the water shut off.

'Shit. I forgot. Err, ok. Hold on.'

'It's ok, I can get it. Carry on.'

'No!'

'Why not? Who are they going to tell?'

'Bola, no. I'm coming.' The buzzer went again. 'Shit. Hold on.'

'It's just a delivery. What was the big deal?' Mona's mobile rang in the bedroom, no doubt they were keen to deliver. 'See. That must be them.' He thought that would quell her fears but it seemed to add to the unprecedented panic.

'No. They'll just come back. Leave it.' Mona opened the bathroom door with her hair still lathered in conditioner and a towel wrapped around her middle. Steam flooded out and the heat hit Bola right in the face.

'Bloody hell. What are you doing in there, boiling pasta?' He looked Mona up and down and saw that her exposed ends were almost as red as a lobster's shell.

'Please just leave it. I'll get them to come back.' Perhaps he wouldn't be staying around today then.

'I don't see what the big deal is, but fine. Your house, your rules.' This seemed to jar Mona a touch and she returned to the bathroom with a huff. He shrugged it off and got back to the kettle and the coffee that was calling. He knew his way around Mona's now, there wasn't much to hide, made an instant and took it back to the bedroom. But one thing did catch his eye: the spare room at the back of the flat. He hadn't actually been in there on the grand tour, Mona had just said it was a spare bedroom. He hesitated while he blew on his coffee, knowing he might have already wound her up somewhat - for what, he didn't know - but Bola was curious by nature. Hell, it was his job to be curious.

Who said you're on shift?

Who's going to be in there, Adrian Hoarding's murderer?

If there even is one.

Bola still hadn't figured that one out. The other suspect was still unknown.

I'm just going to have a look.

Bola could still hear the shower running and figured Mona was still a ways off rinsing all that product out of her hair. He opened the door and saw it was indeed just a spare room. A very messy spare room. No murderer, no satanic figurines or other creepy business. He walked in anyway and started absently picking up the odds and ends that were thrown onto the bed; an assortment of hangers, mostly bent and dusty; light dresses and skirts, that looked like her summer wardrobe; and finally a mix of handbags and small boxes; there didn't seem to be any order in these. Bola saw that the room had built in cupboards, wall to wall.

Does she really not have space for his stuff?

Something started bubbling in his work mind and he struggled to turn it off. Bola popped his head into the corridor to check the shower was still running - it was - then quickly inspected both the cupboards. One contained more clothes, but still had space enough for everything on the bed, the other was completely empty.

Spring clean?

No, that didn't sit right. Mona honestly didn't seem like the kind of person who was that organised or bothered about cleaning. No effort was ever made when he came over.

'Who's she clearing this out for?' he said to himself. Before he knew it Bola started to panic. Was it for him?

Oh you've gone and done it now, she's making room for you buddy.

No, surely not.

They'd only been seeing each other a week - a busy week - but still.

'Fuck. We've seen a lot of each other.' Did Bola need to pump the brakes on this?

Hang on, don't be hasty. Isn't this a good thing?

Is it?

Bola closed up the cupboard and quickly made for Mona's bedroom but struck his foot on something hard that was sticking out from under the bed. His cup of coffee lurched forward in his hand and a few drops escaped and peppered the cream carpet.

'Shit.'

Scooping the bottom of the cup with his hand to catch any more drops he moved as fast as he dared to the kitchen with a brief stop at the bathroom - still showering. He filled up a glass with water, grabbed a kitchen towel and headed back - still showering. He dropped to his knees in the spare room and started to pat and dilute the coffee trying to cover his tracks. Why was he so panicked? He looked across to the bed and saw it was a small suitcase he'd stumbled over. He shook his head aimlessly while he cleaned but his attention was brought back to the suitcase time and time again while he patted, dabbed and panicked. That's not Mona's suitcase, a perceptive part of him thought. He wasn't saying all women had hot pink suitcases with fluffy handles, but there was something distinctly out of place about that little suitcase: it didn't belong here. He was unable to stop himself piecing together the odd behaviour of the delivery, the state of this room, the empty wardrobes and the suitcase.

That fucking suitcase, what was it about that suitcase?

Bola set his cleaning tools aside and pulled it out. It was heavy. He checked around the outside and saw a collection of remarkably ordered city stickers, the spacing was faultless. It looked to have been right around the world, but there was one that caught his eye: Paris.

Bola had spoken to Mona about his brief childhood in France. She had said how she'd always wanted to go to Paris. So why the sticker?

This isn't hers.

Before he could investigate further his ears picked up a distinct lack of a shower at work. He put the suitcase back as he found it and concluded he'd done the best clean up he could in here. He should get himself back into the designated areas. Bola ended up staying for another couple of hours but he struggled to think of anything else but that suitcase.

33

Caz stood in their bedroom, pulling her dressing gown tight around her looking at the black dress, the one exclusively reserved for funerals, which lay on the bed. She pulled her gown even tighter in an attempt to squeeze herself out from the middle like toothpaste, so she could slip away and disappear. Even though Adrian was in the bathroom right now, her brain was still struggling with the reality of this unreal situation.

Questions were buzzing around her head. *How* would today pan out *would* she break down *should* she break down to keep face *could* all the secrets come spilling out? Would the funeral directors smell a rouse? Caz allowed herself to imagine a world where Adrian would pop out the coffin like a Jack-in-a-box. Champagne would flow, music would play and everyone would applaud the prank they had played on this little town. Both detectives would carry in a huge cake with Caz and Adrian's smirking faces, a "gotcha" handwritten in sweet blood red icing underneath. Then Dead Dave would walk in from the sidelines to more applause, removing his Adrian-like prosthetics and spitting out some fake blood capsules. Then everything would return to normal.

Fuck sake.

They could have called this whole thing off if it wasn't for Teddy. "Adrian must continue to be dead." he had said at the end of his first visit. "The whole world could be in danger."

'Fuck sake.'

Caz drove to the cemetery alone where a small service had been planned in the chapel. Mona, Adrian and Caz had discussed the ceremony at length and how much should be done to make it look believable, because they *were* too deep now. They were going for a quick turn around, low key, "shame funeral". Sad that a wife had lost her husband, but ashamed at the fact he was found dead somewhere he shouldn't have been, doing something he probably shouldn't have been doing. Caz had made this clear on the phone to those who called, with her now well practised bouts of broken voice and sniffles until the caller felt uncomfortable enough to hang up. They'd decided to stop answering the door altogether, their security cameras telling them all they needed to know. Caz's route was clear as day – no traffic or railway crossings to slow her down. She'd made the trip north of town in what felt like record time. Any hope of a delay or broken down vehicle was scuppered. The universe wanted this day to happen.

Fuck sake.

She dropped the car into second and shut Freddie

Mercury up mid-chorus on the stereo as she passed the threshold into the cemetery. It was a subconscious sign of respect she had learnt from her parents when they used to visit her grandparents' graves.

It was rather beautiful here. Furlong Cemetery sat on the foot of the Downs, and from the top there was a nice view of the town. A good place for *the long sleep*. She wound through the narrow road with the dead flanking her sides. Her engine rumbled, the echoes bouncing sequentially off the stone cold headstones.

Caz cut her engine as she pulled into a parking space next to the chapel. She let her hands drop off the wheel and sink back into her lap. The silence unnerved her. Just a minute then she'd head inside. Mona's car was there, as well as others, but she was unsure of their owners. An uneasy feeling crept into her stomach, like she was being watched, judged. Was it the dead, tutting six feet under at this facade of a funeral? Or something else, something... official. Her senses had certainly been heightened during this fiasco, but she wouldn't claim she suddenly had a sixth scene - although such things seemed possible now that parallel universes apparently existed.

Do exist. Remember, you felt them.

She looked into the distance. There were two women up by a headstone on her left, one sweeping away at something on the headstone, the other watching with her crossed arms trying to keep warm. A single man stood a couple of headstones down, again not looking at Caz, but preoccupied with the headstone in front of him. She looked to the right and saw two people a little further away between headstones. They weren't looking down at any headstones, in fact their heads were pointing straight at

Caz. She didn't have the plot layout of the cemetery in her head, but she'd been there enough to know they stood where there wasn't any room for new arrivals. They were standing in turn of the century stuff. Who would be buried there? A great, great, great grandparent? Were they police?

They're here to arrest me, she thought.

Maybe that would be easier, Turner.

Before she could panic further, a puff of smoke issued from one of their mouths, the words lost to the bitter wind, and they turned on their heels and walked off. Any other day, Caz wouldn't have thought this odd, in fact, she wouldn't have even looked around. She'd never been so paranoid.

Fuck sake.

The tiny congregation ceased its talking when Caz entered, they all rose to their feet out of respect. A closed coffin already rested at the altar and Caz's stomach clenched as if expecting a punch from Adrian's ghost. Caz hadn't wanted to follow the coffin in. After much debate, they had decided burying was the best option so they could later reveal to the police there were indeed two Adrian's. It was the best way to keep any business of perverting the course of justice to a minimum and Adrian wouldn't stop threatening about the potential consequences of burning his other half and the link to spontaneous combustion. Either way, this wasn't going to be easy. She felt hot.

Mona arrived at her side for support. Caz wasn't quite sure how this rollercoaster would go but she knew she needed Mona. If Adrian had really died, Mona would be at her side. Their parents both died when Mona and Caz were in their mid twenties. Their father died of a very aggressive prostate cancer and their mother shortly after from nothing short of a broken heart. She had been completely unresponsive following the loss of her husband. Each day it seemed a part of her was dying, like a tree shedding its leaves – each one with a piece of her heart attached until there was nothing left. Mona and Caz hadn't been able to shake their mother out of her stupor and before they knew it, just the two of them were left. Caz then inherited the matriarch title, population: two. Now she thought of it, she'd hadn't attended a funeral since - although this was debatable as a real funeral. At least their parent's absence made this lie a little easier.

Mona had taken her hand in hers and was looking for reassurance herself. Mona took the sorrow for the both of them when it had been their parents, Caz took the reins. Mona had always been more sensitive, but it was never a nuisance, that's how it had always been. Caz simply tried not to think too much about the death of their parents. Caz tried to relax, but this all felt like a horrible rehearsal for a day she never wanted to come.

They had managed to keep family numbers down to just three on account of the fact few were in the country. The late notice of the funeral date was a deliberate ploy targeted at those concerned. Mona and Caz had outright not told their surviving aunties and uncles. They never spoke anyway. The passing of their parents had created canyons, not bridges - so much for stepping up - but she fobbed it off with the fact they weren't orphaned children in need of a roof over their heads. Would they have stepped up then, she thought? The situation was unearthing lots of old questions that she tried to push aside.

Not now.

Adrian's side wasn't too complicated either thankfully

- as thankful as you could be for dead parents. His mother, who had raised Adrian and his sister single handedly, had passed away only a few years back. She had no siblings. That meant Adrian only had three family members in attendance today; his sister, Pam - also a single mother - and her two children. Why had both their parents died so young?

Not now, Turner.

Had their barren families stuck Adrian and Caz together? Was isolation their greatest connection?

Stop it!

Caz thought about the silence of the South Downs, that sat just outside the chapel, and gave some serious thought to scarpering into them as Pam approached.

Caz had let them into the house just once since the incident and she hadn't allowed them back since. His sister was absolutely beside herself when she had visited, and the kids had regressed into new-born babies with tears and snot cascading out their little faces like waterfalls. Caz had never been very good with children and had to tend to them while Pam sat with a glass of gin she'd poured herself on entering. They'd spoken on the phone a few times since, but playing the grieving wife had its benefits and Caz had managed to keep her at bay ever since.

'Caz,' Pam said, shaking off the children and embracing Caz in a tight hug. Caz still wasn't sure how to play along.

'How are...' She trailed off, adjusting her words, then flapping her hand in front of her face to try and waft the tears back into her body.

'Thank you, Pam,' Caz said. 'Once all this is over we can get back to normal.'

Pam nodded at this despite looking a little hurt, as though Caz was trying to wave this whole thing off like a bad smell - which is exactly what she was trying to do. In a panic, she tried to strain her face into some kind of grief but knew she didn't have the acting talent, so instead embraced Pam once again and managed some fake sobs into her heavy jacket. Pam squeezed back. The softness returned to Pam's face after this second embrace. She gave Mona a quick hug then headed back down the aisle to her seat, Adrian's awkward little nephews following.

Mona gave Caz a little pat and nod. Then came the friends. Caz had also kept them at bay with the same act, but more so because she hadn't completely trusted Adrian to not break the safety of the attic and let them in on the secret. One after the other, they gave their condolences, and after the fourth, she genuinely broke down. The mix of heartfelt condolences, the looks on their faces, the fact they were genuinely grieving for Adrian, became too much. It struck her for the first time that she didn't have the hardest job today – it was them. The poor sods who thought Adrian was actually dead. What were they going to do when they found out? Would they be mad they had kept it a secret? Would they understand? Or would they never know? She felt exhausted after the conga line of condolences had passed, and made her way to the front with Mona at her side.

The funeral celebrant, who Caz had only spoken to on the phone, approached and squeezed Caz's shoulder. They had been through the ceremony in advance. Caz said she wouldn't be speaking and wanted it all done by the celebrant in a quick, respectable manner. And it was. There were silences at the right times, sobs at the right times, a respectful simmer of laughter, then the music played: Crocodile Rock by Elton John, Adrian's choice. "Darling, I must be the only person in the world who can get feedback on their funeral song choice," he had said.

Caz looked around and it seemed to have had the desired effect. Smiles and polite laughter. Perhaps it was a little reassurance that everything was going to be ok.

34

'I don't know if the court will go for this Bola,' Kim said, looking at the application for a warrant. It was fluffy to say the least.

'We still don't know who that other suspect was, do we?' he said.

'No, you don't need to tell me that. But they won't grant you a warrant for your ignorance.' She flipped through the sheet again, trying to look at it objectively. 'And why her sister's house? They'll want to know,'

'Because any evidence that might have been there will be gone by now. You were right, the doorstepping showed that something was up and I get the impression she's smart enough to get rid of anything incriminating. I've made a note of that visit and I'll explain to the judge,'

'What could she have removed, a murder weapon?' Kim asked.

'Come on.'

'I'm just playing court.

'I think we know she didn't kill him. But there's a

good chance she was that second person at Marsh Avenue,' Bola said.

'You aren't thinking of a DNA request too are you? That would be–'

'Pointless, I know,' Bola cut across. 'Having your spouse's DNA on your forehead is hardly grounds for arrest. I just need to get into her sister's place.'

Kim studied Bola. He hadn't asked for any help lately and she only got news when she asked for it. Ultimately, this is what she had wanted. She was too busy to get as involved as she had been at the start. He seemed straight in his answers, but it almost felt rehearsed. She thought back to the day when Bola and Mona had bumped into each other and the story Bola had recounted. She just hoped there was nothing in it. If Bola had somehow started things up again she would have one shitstorm on her hands. Disciplinaries, internal reports, suspensions - then she'd be even more short staffed. She pried further.

'What do you know, Bola?'

'It's not what I know. It's what I suspect. I believe there's incriminating evidence at Miss. Turner's house that could help us with the investigation.'

'OK, say there *is* evidence there. What would this evidence look like? What are we looking for?'

'I don't know exactly–'

'Bola. I am being serious now. What are you looking for? I am not taking this to the magistrates. You're reaching.'

'Adrian's belongings.'

'What?'

'I believe Caz and Mona are working together to cover something up. They're hiding some of Adrian's belongings

- the kind of things they don't want others to know about - at her house. Be that tools of the trade for burglaries, some kind of data theft, identify theft tools. Illegally obtained or otherwise illegal to possess. Perhaps even drugs.'

'You think the three of them are career criminals?'

'Potentially on the side, yes. Something went wrong at Marsh and they're scrambling to cover.'Bola knew more than he was letting on. He knew exactly what he was looking for. How he knew that was a question Kim didn't want to know the answer to, but she had to ask.

'Are you seeing Ramona Turner again?'

'What? No. Of course not.' His face gave nothing away. If he had suspected that question he'd at least been prepared to hide any shock or guilt.

'Do I need to tell you the consequences of such things?'

'I'm aware, thank you boss. I wouldn't sabotage the case.'

Boss? He's fucking her. He's bloody fucking her.

'How certain are you that you'll find something there?' Kim asked.

'I'll put my job on it,' Bola said.

You are putting your job on it mate.

What should she do? She could push this through and get their cases down, something told her Bola would actually get it closed with this final step. But it was still early in the game. Most investigations of this sort stretched out for months. The warrant could take weeks - unless she used her connections to expedite it. She'd used them for less in the past. There were also standard clauses that allowed for faster processes if evidence was at risk. Risk. What was the risk in applying?

'What's the harm in applying?' Bola said, seeming to read Kim's mind.

'Get out of my head.'

'Huh?'

'Nothing. I know where you're coming from. But there are still risks, I don't want internal investigations around defective applications.'

'Every county has defective applications. It's the judges that say yes. What's one more?'

'Bola. May I remind you that you're speaking to a superior and your cavalier attitude and opinions are not making you look like a credible detective at this moment.' Kim let that settle while Bola struggled for words. She'd never had to put Bola in his place before. He had something, that much was sure. He wouldn't be pushing it this much otherwise.

'I'm sorry,' he said. 'We don't have much, but this is a step in the right direction. We could be having this conversation next month, asking for a warrant down the line. Why not at least apply now then we can sit on it. We have what, three months to execute?'

'It depends what they grant you.'

'Right. We may never use it,' Bola said, finishing his case. What was the harm, Kim thought?

That inbox is looking pretty full darling.

Kim flicked to the back of the application and signed. Bola didn't gloat. He thanked her and returned to his desk.

35

It was raining hard and Mona was trying to keep herself out of Adrian's way with a new book. He had been in Mona's flat for less than twenty-four hours and he was already jittery. He was fussing over the littlest things, constantly asking Mona questions about where things went, he used the bathroom at least twenty times a day. Was he this bad at home, she thought?

Mona hadn't necessarily wanted Adrian to move in. The solution had wiggled onto the table and, clearly seeing the stress Caz was under after the prying visitation from the police, Mona had agreed to take him in for a time. Mona and Adrian got on fine, but they wouldn't have been friends outside of her sister's marriage. He got on her nerves for the most part. He was petulant and reminded Mona of some of her students. It was hard to get a straight answer out of him and that's if you could hold his attention. He always gave the impression he had somewhere else to be. Somewhere more important. She also regularly caught him staring at her breasts, petty, but annoying.

Yes, they are attached and they belong to me, thank you very much Mr. Brother-in-law. Mona knew he'd never do anything more than stare. He was just being a man and Caz had had worse men in the past. Better the devil you know.

Get back to your book and forget about that brat!

Her heroine had just stumbled over an odd piece of metal on her land and she was already giddy to know what madness her favourite author had cooked up this time. Before Mona could even find the sentence again the buzzer went off for her door. Adrian was in her face like a shot.

'Who's that?' he said.

'I don't know. Just leave it.' This didn't seem to comfort him, 'People are always hitting the wrong buzzer. There's four flats in this house.'

'Right,' he said without moving.

It buzzed a second time.

'Yes, I heard it.' Mona snapped before Adrian could open his mouth again. 'Just, go wait in your room or something. You're making me nervous standing there.'

'We didn't think about this. There's nowhere to hide here.'

'Adrian. Relax. Who's it going to be? No one knows you're here. No one even knows you're alive. I can turn whoever it is away.'

'Not if it's the police.'

'Well I think I can even do that unless they have a warrant, right? Anyway, just relax. Go, go, go.'

Adrian was scratching the cut on his head that her dear sister had given him. It was going to scar horribly.

'Fine. Let's look out the window shall we?' Mona tossed her book aside and looked out to the front. Her heart hammered instantly at what she saw.

There were four police officers at the end of her drive standing like sentinels in the rain.

'Oh fuck,' she said.

'What?'

'Hide.'

'Hide?'

The buzzer went again followed by some knocks that were heard up on her floor.

'What the fuck are we going to do?' Adrian said, 'Why did we think this was a good idea?'

'Relax,' Mona said again.

'Stop telling–'

'Adrian, just fucking shut up! I can handle this.' Could she? Sure, it'll probably be Bola just playing a joke. 'I know the detective.'

'Know the detective? How?'

'Adrian. Just go to your room.'

'I'm going out the window,' he said, his feet skidding out beneath him.

'Window? It's not like you've killed anyone, you idiot.'

How bad would this turn out, Mona thought? How did it get to this? She could have stopped all of this had she just got out of her car and gone into the station. Hell, she could have phoned. All this madness, it could have all been avoided.

The buzzer went once more. She snatched it off the wall.

'Yes!'

'Miss. Ramona Turner,' said the voice. It was Bola and he was being official.'I'm Detective Bola Cassin. I have a warrant here to search your premises as part of an ongoing investigation into the death of Mr. Adrian Hoarding.'

Fuck.

'Hello? Miss. Turner?'

'Yes.'

'Do you understand?'

'Yes.'

'Can you please open your door or we will have to force entry.'

'Yes.'

Mona tried to steady her breathing and fathom how much of a fuck up this was. Would she be in trouble too? Big trouble?

She sighed and buzzed the door open while she heard banging in Adrian's room. Within seconds there was banging at her main door.

Bola stood in the doorway flanked by two other officers. He handed over a slip of paper without so much as a smile - they were no longer lovers. Mona glossed over it but didn't really take the images or the words in. The paper felt like it was made of lead.

'Do you understand what this means? We will be searching your property now. Is there anything in your property you would like to tell me about now?'

Mona was not her sister. She didn't carry the same wit. Caz could have kept them at bay until the cows came home. Mona, however, was lost for words and managed little more than a feeble nod.

'Ok. I would ask you to wait outside, but seeing as it's raining,' A small mercy from her ex-lover, 'could I please ask you to take a seat inside out of the way.'

'I...' Mona started. She wasn't sure what to do. Did Adrian manage to get out the window - he was a good climber. Could she keep Bola at bay by announcing their relationship, would it void the warrant? The three of them grossly misjudged where the police were casting their net. Could she get out of this? Would she throw her sister under the bus?

Mona!

But wait, she hadn't done anything wrong. She hadn't killed Adrian, there was no blood on her hands. Adrian wasn't even dead! This whole thing had been blown out of proportion due to the fact Caz and Adrian were concerned about a murderer that, for all they knew, didn't exist. But she'd wrapped herself up in all this too. Maybe this was what needed to happen. Maybe this needed to come out so they could get on with their lives.

Bola looked back at her, waiting for her to spill something. She could sense that's what he wanted. What did he know? Did I let something slip while we were together, she thought? After a moment, he turned to the officers and signalled them to head in. He removed his hat, politely flicked the rain off through the door, and pushed past her without a further word.

'Police. Police,' he shouted into the flat. 'Is anyone else in the property?'

Mona flinched and made her way into her living room. She heard claws clicking on her laminate floorboards and soon a little spaniel whizzed past her with the officer struggling a little to keep hold of the lead.

'You're sure no one else is here?' he asked one more time. He was giving her plenty of opportunities to come forward but her mind was already rushing through what Adrian was now up to. Did those windows open wide enough? She decided to keep quiet. They would undoubtedly find him and she'd have to get a lawyer, that's how these things worked. Best not to say anything that could harm her defence. She put her head in her hands. She didn't care that she looked guilty. There was nothing she could do now.

'Darren, start in the kitchen with Pepsi,' said the detective. The man with the dog nodded and began leading the spaniel to the kitchen.

'Sophie, watch the door. Zina, stay here with Miss. Turner.' Neither responded with words but took up their positions as directed. Bola went back into the hallway followed by another shout out, 'Police. Is anyone here?' he boomed.

Mona heard doors open; he was in her bedroom - a room he was very familiar with. Was he just using her this whole time, she thought?

Bastard.

She tried again to picture available hiding spots but the footsteps were already leaving her room. She didn't have a big flat. He must be checking the bathroom now – there was nowhere to hide in there. At least this wouldn't take long.

'Sophie, with me,' Bola said.

More footsteps through the flat. Even though she had much bigger things to worry about right then, she couldn't help but concern herself with the officer's wet boots.

She heard the final door open to the spare bedroom. He

would be doing one of two things now: trying to squeeze through a window the size of a small painting, or hiding under the bed. She closed her eyes and waited for the inevitable.

36

Adrian lay under the metal bed frame. He'd just about managed to crawl under from the side. He tried to steady his breath as much as possible - for a dead man who wasn't dead. His heart was thudding with an unrelenting force. Perhaps it was beating hard in an attempt to be heard, to betray its master and get caught, putting an end to this daily torment of cortisol it had to ship round the body.

Come on, let's turn ourselves in. We know there's no killer. Give up this nightmare you're living. Feel the wind in your hair again before it all falls out.

If the thumping heart wasn't enough, his legs had started to quiver under the stress. He focused on a stain in the carpet and tried to relax his muscles. It seemed his whole body was trying to double-cross him. He'd bet his legs would have walked him down to the police station if they knew where they were going. Adrian still thought daily about turning himself in. He constantly had to remind himself he wasn't a criminal, despite living like one.

Adrian's crimes of perverting justice, however, were getting worse by the day.

The longer they left it, the greater the punishment would surely be for wasting police time. He wasn't clued up on all the laws around this kind of thing, but he knew all three of them were in trouble. Why had they spun this out? They'd rushed a bloody funeral and everything. They *looked* guilty now. Why had they done that, surely that would have been the moment to pull the plug. If only the police had been on the other side of that door instead of Teddy. But where would they be now? Teddy had said the world could be in danger and to play along. How exactly it was in danger he'd now demand an answer for.

Adrian felt as if the legs of the bed were getting shorter, the weight of the lies soon to trap him. Could he distract the police before they reached his room? How quickly could he get a good old fashioned bomb scare going? He awkwardly slipped his new phone out of his pocket to dial 999 and activate this mad chain of thoughts. Just as he unlocked his phone, he heard one of the police officers outside the door.

'Sophie, with me,' came a male voice from outside the door.

Two thuds struck the bedroom door, the kind executed by a tightly clenched side fist. The hinges whined.

'Police. Is anyone in there?'

The door didn't have a lock, but clearly the only closed door had raised the hackles of the detective outside. The handle turned and the door swung open, bouncing against the wall of the bedroom. Adrian saw two pairs of feet enter cautiously. One owner wore polished police issue boots.

The other wore smart buckled shoes, unpolished and scuffed lightly with chalk.

Adrian looked at his phone again, the wild bomb scare plan out the window. Caz smiled up at him from the wallpaper he'd set before moving into Mona's. His beautiful and quick-witted Caz. He hoped her punishment wouldn't be as severe. He'd throw himself down in front of the judge to soak up any and all of her wrongdoing. Adrian wasn't sure if the photo of Caz had telepathically passed some quick wit on to him, but he'd had one last stroke of... he wasn't sure if it was brilliance, but he'd soon see.

He quickly swiped up his note-taking app and typed the first thing that came to mind. "Parallel universes. I'm the real Adrian. Other Adrian died in transit." Would the detective buy this? It wasn't a lie but it was a lot to expect of someone. Would the sight of Adrian alone, alive and well, be enough to get the detective on side? There was no better time to explain. He added one more line. "Come back alone - WORLD IN DANGER!!!!" Adrian pinched and rotated the screen to make it as easy to read as possible.

'Watch my back,' said the detective. The chalky shoes came to rest at the foot of the bed. Adrian knew what was coming. Adrian flipped the phone around and held it out to be read by the detective. He put on his most law abiding citizen smile and prayed to the universe.

Please work.

Adrian saw a pair of knees, followed by hands, then a face. His immediate thoughts were that the detective was more handsome than he'd imagined. Somehow, his mind allowed him to wonder if Caz had omitted this detail when describing the detective to him. When their eyes met, Adrian felt an odd sense of relief.

It's all over now.

The detective clearly didn't share this relief as he instantly screamed and recoiled at the sight of Adrian.

'What is it?' the other officer said, getting down to her knees.

The detective went to open his mouth, then Adrian saw his eyes focus on the mobile screen and take the message in. Would he play by the book? The detective looked back at Adrian, kindness gone. He had transmitted a message of warning, one that should not be taken lightly. *You fuck with me, I will rip you apart. You run, I will find you, then rip you apart.*

'Bloody shopping bag,' the detective said, as cool as a cucumber. 'It's got a fucking face on it. Caught me off guard,' he said whilst getting up from the floor.

Ok, that's smart.

Adrian saw the polished boots shuffle towards the bed. 'Ha, let's have a look.'

'No,' came the detective's voice once more, authority rooted in it. 'Get back to the front door. I'll check the wardrobe. We're good here.'

The boots promptly took themselves out of the room and back downstairs. The latest member of the biggest kept secret in town slowly closed the door and calmly walked back to the bed.

'Phone,' he said. 'Now.'

This had gone a million times better than Adrian had planned. The secret was safe, for the time being. Was the world really in danger as Teddy had said? Surely, having a detective on side was better than the whole police service knowing. Not a bad day in the office for Adrian, or was he getting ahead of himself? He slid the phone out from under the bed but it struck one of the feet.

'Sorry,' Adrian said.

Fuck me. What a week.

The phone was promptly picked up. Adrian's mind began to wander about the motives of this detective. Adrian allowed himself to think only of the positive. He waited for further instruction but none came. The chalky shoes left the room and pulled the door shut. Adrian allowed his body to melt into the carpet. He didn't know what was coming, but this was the best he'd felt in days.

37

'We're going to jail aren't we?' Caz said to Adrian over her car's Bluetooth. She was stuck at the crossings, of course. She let out a scream. An old couple waiting by the barriers on foot heard her and looked around. They were wrapped in their matching black parkas, their old wrinkled heads poking out the top. Caz shot them a look. They raised their eyebrows, then turned back to the crossing.

'I dunno,' Adrian said. 'I'm not cuffed in the back of the van. I'd say the outlook is only bleak, not catastrophic. I tried to hide, but you know Mona's place. It was either under the bed or in the wardrobe, so I took the bed. He was going to find me either way, and luckily the other officer didn't know I was there. He told them to go straight away. He was pretty sharp.'

The police must have smelt something funny for a while now – there were processes to follow for a warrant? But to go straight to Mona's, what were they looking for? Had they known Adrian would be there? Did they know he was alive, or had it been a surprise for everyone?

'Sneaky fuckers,' she said.

'Sharp, sneaky fuckers,' Adrian replied.

'Those bloody detectives. I knew something was up, but I thought they'd come back to our house. All this time they've been quiet, they've been planning this. They've had me on their hit list. How could I have been so stupid? What are they going to do, Adrian?'

'I don't know.'

'Were both the detectives there?'

'No. It was just the guy, and from what Mona told me, a bunch of bobbies in uniform.'

'Bobbies?'

'Yeah, like plain clothed offi—'

'I know what a bloody bobby is, Adrian.'

'Well, why'd you ask?' Adrian said.

'I was being facetious. I've never heard you call a police officer a bobby. Stop speaking like a criminal. We haven't done anything wrong, I didn't kill you. You didn't kill you, we need to remember that.'

'Alright, alright. I know, Caz. I have to keep reminding myself we're not murderers and it's *me* that's dead. We've been sneaking around like criminals since that night. I feel guilty. Someone *did* die and that might still cause issues. To the police, a dead body is a dead body, and they'll still want to find out what happened, apprehend anyone that needs apprehending, and close the case. You know who that means.'

'Fucking Teddy.' Caz thudded the steering wheel in anger.

When will this train come?

'Who's Teddy?' she heard her sister say in the

background, but neither answered her. They were still protecting her.

'We put ourselves in this hole,' Caz continued, thudding the wheel harder with each syllable.

'We are in a hole, yes.' Adrian's voice came calmly over the line. 'But this detective, he may have just sent down a ladder to get us out and…Well we've got Mona to thank for that.'

'Please don't drag her into this any more, Adrian.'

'It wasn't me. She wants to talk to you about it. But without her I think the detective might have dragged me off already.'

'How do you mean?' Caz asked.

'She said she'd rather speak to you in person.'

'Adrian, put her on,' Caz said.

'No.'

'Adrian, that is not your decision to make.'

'Why are you being such an arse about this?' he said.

'What?'

'We might have an out from this nightmare and you… you're being unreasonable.'

'We do not have an out!'

'But we have something,' Adrian said,

'We have nothing, Adrian! And what about that end-of-the-world nonsense Teddy warned of? Not telling the police?'

'It could have been bullshit. I don't know how many times I have to explain this to you, Caz. I'm tired. Very, very tired. You have been there, but you have absolutely no idea how hard this has been for me. You're not the one playing dead. All the sneaking, the hiding, the being locked inside. Everyone thinking I'm dead. I can't even go and stand by the window. I'm fucking sick of it. We should have told the police, we should have been honest from the start. It's not your fault. I admit it was my choice, and I fucked up. I was scared. But God, I wish we hadn't sat on this rollercoaster. We let it go on for too long, then Teddy got in the middle, and I was really starting to think we'd never be able to crawl out of it without some kind of repercussion. Some time in prison for sure. But now we have this life line. This detective knows something's not quite right, he's on our side. I think most people would feel the same if they saw me walking around. How the hell could I be dead *and* alive. This whole thing is fucking nuts. We seem to be the only ones who can't see that. We're literally too close to this.'

Caz listened to the words while the lights of the barriers blinked away, now not even caring they were still down. She knew he was right. They'd made the wrong choices.

'I'm sorry Adrian. I should have...' She really didn't know.

'It's ok,' Adrian said.

There was no use trying to pin the blame on any one person. They just had to concede it was nuts. And poor Mona, they had dragged her into this too.

'How's Mona?' Caz asked.

'Let me talk to her now,' Mona said in the background. Caz heard the phone being passed.

'Hey,' Mona said over the line.

Caz's stomach panged. Her poor sister. She'd never forgive herself if she also came under fire for this. Caz was meant to be her protector. That was her job since their parents had passed.

'Hey. You ok?' Caz replied.

'Yes. Yes, I'm fine.'

'Mona I'm so sorry.'

'Don't be. I got myself involved just as much with the viewing and all that. The police were fine. They're just outside the house now. My neighbours are getting quite a view. There's a dog and everything. I don't know if we should be speaking to you really. He took Adrian's phone, but not mine. We don't know what's happening now.'

'Mona, I don't think we ever knew what was *really* happening.'

'Yeah. Guess so.'

'So what's this about you helping, what did you do? You didn't do anything silly did you? Didn't confess?'

'Well, it's a bit of a mess really. An accident, but a mess. I said I was too involved. But maybe I did help somehow.'

'What did you do, Mona?'

'Not what,' Mona said.

'Not what? Don't tell me it's a who. Mona. You didn't? The detective? Again? How could…When?' Mona had explained why that meeting at the house had been awkward, but how had they rekindled and why hadn't she told her? What had happened to their trust? Caz nearly exploded but she was too overwhelmed with the new developments.

'Well, I hate to fight fire with fire but I've questions for you too,' Mona said.

'I don't think so missy–' Before Caz could get going Mona cut across. She'd had the bullet in the chamber all along.

'Who's Teddy, Caz?'

38

Bola looked at the officers making sure they understood his instructions: stay put, don't come in. He hadn't told them what he'd found, although Sophie did seem suspicious after he'd dismissed her. He said he was just questioning the suspect, which was true - the other officers just didn't know there were two of them. He saw a lot of young faces eager to please and not to question. 'Got it?' he said, in his most authoritative tone.

'Yes, sir,' came a fairly enthusiastic but offbeat reply from the faces. It reminded him of a school assembly. He walked back up the path to the house.

Bola knew there was something off about that suitcase. He had quietly phoned a contact at the foreign office and got a report of Adrian's movements for the past decade. He was quite the jet-setter. The destinations matched the neatly arranged stickers he had seen on the heavy suitcase. It was a flimsy piece of evidence at best - they were related after all - but Bola had been right nonetheless. He just hadn't expected to be right in this way. Adrian was still alive.

He was giddy to unravel this one, but he wouldn't be showing his excitement to the suspects inside. Bola's early lessons of trusting suspects and victims rang heavy in his ears - what was he playing at? - but they were completely devoured by his overwhelming sense of curiosity and the phrase he had read on the phone: Parallel Universes. Bola was familiar with the concept in Hollywood form, but surely it wasn't real. DNA confirmed Adrian was dead, officers had confirmed that Adrian's funeral had gone ahead, and the body had been buried. So, who was *that* hiding under the bed? Where did Mona sit in all of this, was it perhaps no coincidence they had bumped into each other again? That they'd slept together, again. Was she playing him? The thought stung Bola somewhat.

No, not Mona. Lovely sweet - sexy - Mona.

If it wasn't for Mona he would have already cuffed that man in the house, Adrian or not, and brought him in.

'I know, I know.' He tried to convince himself he wasn't doing anything stupid. He rubbed his kidney again.

Objectively, Adrian was alive. He was there in that house but…Adrian was also dead. Adrian had no record of a twin. That would have been the simplest way to explain what he'd just seen. The simplest conclusion would be a case of mistaken identity, but there would have been a long trail of fuck ups for that to stick: DNA included. With regards to motive and the secrecy, he was dying to know the reasons. He paused briefly at the front door. If he stepped through now, he wouldn't be playing by the book.

Were you playing by the book all the other times you

stepped through this door? You wouldn't have found that
suitcase if you played by the book.

The first two words he'd read on the phone came
floating into his vision once again - Parallel Universes -
and Bola made his decision.

He pushed open the door, did a perfunctory sweep of
the empty rooms then headed to the back bedroom. Bola
thought about knocking but pushed on through to find
Mona and Adrian sitting on the foot of the bed. They
looked like naughty school children. Why did everything
remind him of school today?

'If you could make your way to the top of the bed, feet
on the mattress.' Bola wanted to have the advantage if
anything physical were to happen, although the collapsible
nightstick under his jacket gave him extra confidence. He
waited for them to settle, then took up his position at the
foot of the bed. He didn't take out a notepad or recorder –
this would stay off record for now. He just wanted
answers.

'I trust neither of you are going to try anything stupid?'

They silently shook their heads. He directed his next
question straight at Adrian, and there was no doubt it *was*
Adrian.

'Name?'

There was a brief moment of composure from Adrian
but then he spoke. 'Adrian Hoarding.'

'And the body at Marsh Avenue? The one your wife
identified, whose DNA we swabbed and whose body we
cut open. Who was that?' Bola asked.

'Well. Me. Adrian Hoarding.'

'Bullshit,' Bola said. He wasn't quite sure why he said
that, or quite so quickly. He knew there would be some

explanation, but it caught him off guard nonetheless. He tried to settle and returned to the questioning.

'It was another me. From a parallel universe,' Adrian added.

'Come on. I'm risking my job here and you're going to spin me this shit? Why was your car outside thirty-three Marsh Avenue? Was that from a parallel universe too? Mona, what is this?'

'It's the truth. I know this sounds nuts, but it was me. There's this scientist. He's figured–'

'Trying to claim insurance money?' Bola cut in.

'What? No. We haven't even phoned them yet.'

'Yet?'

'That's not what I meant.'

'Scam artist, this science guy, is he? Told you he could fake your death, pay off your mortgage?' Bola wanted to keep pushing and jumping erratically around until something snapped.

'What on earth are you on about?' Adrian said.

'Not the first time it's been done. Bloody good show you've put –'

'There is no show! I don't even know what's going on. But I am alive. Can't you see that?'

Bola enjoyed making people crack in questioning. Half the work was normally done for him with non-career criminals; they sweated the moment they were confronted by a detective. Even innocent people on the road drove oddly when they saw a police car in their rear view.

'Evidence?' Bola asked.

'*I* am your evidence. Look at *me*!'

'So who killed the other guy?'

'We didn't kill anyone!' Mona said.

'Oh, so you *are* tied up in this are you?' Most likely, they were all in it together, but Bola still couldn't complete the puzzle.

'I wanted to tell you. Honestly Bola. It's been killing me.'

'Really? It's a bit convenient isn't it? Strangers in the night then we bump into each other with all this going on. Are you trying to manipulate me?' This was both an official and personal question.

'No, no. We don't even know what's going on. Well at least I think we didn't. I've only just found out about this Teddy.'

'Mona, we didn't tell you—' Adrian started.

'To protect me, I know. But it didn't work. You should have let me know. Maybe Bola could have helped.'

'Then, why are you living together?' Bola asked, with his hands held out wide. His jacket fell open at this and he saw Adrian's eyes dart to the collapsible nightstick hooked into his belt. Good, Bola thought. Take a look.

'Because…' Adrian started, he looked like he was about to cry. All that stress and anguish. Bola didn't have a shred of sympathy.

That's what happens when you try and cover up a murder.

Adrian was apparently at a loss for words.

'Was that even a real body? How did you get the DNA to match? Is it some failed clone experiment?'

'It's another me. I said parallel universes. I'm not making it up. My phone. Can I have it?'

'Who do you need to call?' Bola asked.

'No one. There's a video. Maybe that will be easier.'

'What video?' Mona said.

'I'm sorry,' Adrian said, turning on the bed to Mona. 'We were trying to keep you safe from all this… nonsense.' He reached out to comfort her but she recoiled. It was all falling apart now. Self-preservation was a bitch. Bola obliged and took Adrian's phone out. Adrian held out his hand to receive it but Bola wasn't falling for that.

'Uh, uh. What's your code?' Bola said.

'1111,' Adrian said.

'Inventive,' Bola said as he punched the numbers in. The phone unlocked with a click. At least that saves a job for the cyber team later, he thought. He realised the phone had no signal and was in aeroplane mode. It seemed Adrian knew a thing or two about staying off the radar; his guilty habits were starting to show. It was a risky game for a dead man to carry a phone. However, they hadn't been looking for Adrian. They had been looking for his killer.

'Go to videos,' Adrian said.

'What am I looking for?'

'It'll be the only one,' Adrian said what appeared to be his final piece and then put his head in his hands. Bola heard Mona curse Adrian for something, but he was already watching the video and shortly after didn't care about anything else but that. Something told him it wasn't a fake.

39

Teddy sat on the ground in the alley behind Marsh Avenue. The cold was deep in his bones, but he had to be sure of his calculations. He was out of sight behind a privet bush that had put up a good fight against the bitter winter and retained most of its leaves, even if they were a little yellow. The bridge to other worlds was still working. Teddy could feel the effects and tuning into the bridge's pushes and pulls had become easier now he understood the feelings better. He seemed to have found a good distance down the alley where he could handle the nauseating push and resist the tempting pull. Knowledge was certainly power, Teddy thought.

What Teddy had managed to prove via physical experimentation was that the bridge swapped between each scenario sequentially roughly every ninety minutes, and the push segments outweighed the pull and silence segments by three to one. Thankfully, it wasn't built on possibilities like quantum mechanics was, if it had been random there would be too many moving parts. As such,

Teddy was able to detect both the type of connection the bridge had and where it was in its sequence.

Teddy had three test subjects: Caz, Adrian and himself. He knew the states the bridge had been in for each of them based on the feelings they had described when they had trespassed in search of answers. It was simple maths to work backwards in ninety minute segments, and Adrian's push symptoms on the night of travel confirmed Teddy's theory. Therefore, he knew his own sequence down to the tenth of a second, Adrian's to the second and Caz's to the minute. Teddy was thankful for this as it made his plan simpler. He was going to use the bridge to coax Adrian in and keep Caz away. Adrian wouldn't be able to resist if he felt the intensity from inside the house. Nothing would break the attraction if he acted within the sequence window.

What happened to Adrian if you're so sure?

No one can know everything. That is why we exist!

You could lose him again.

Not this time.

Teddy knew there was a strong chance that the bridge wouldn't take them back to *his* world. This didn't upset him. It had always been a strong possibility, and he and Adrian had only briefly discussed possible solutions to this issue. They had been so hell-bent on looking forward, they hadn't paid much attention to returning to the world they were leaving behind. It didn't matter where they ended up, it would be a phenomenal experience. This world wasn't as similar as they had theorised, perhaps there were even wilder alternatives out there as Adrian had fantasised about; flying cars, aliens on Earth. It was all theoretically possible. Teddy sat there with his stomach turning over in the push, smiling at the memories of Adrian – *his* Adrian.

'Soon,' he said quietly.

What if this Adrian isn't the same?

A blackbird chirped its final song of the day in a nearby tree, the overcast sky soaking up the last of the sun as it faded to black. Teddy checked his watch. It was just coming up to ninety minutes – the next turn of the bridge.

Then I'll find another.

He pulled out his new phone in preparation for the call to Caz. He was surprised she had given him her number, but she had certainly changed her manners towards him since she had seen the opportunity to be rid of him once and for all.

And if that one doesn't love you either?

It was a selfish act – her own motives at the core of the offer – but was Teddy any different? Teddy was playing them both, and it was making a hell of a racket in his head. It was like a John Cage symphony, specially composed for this moment, and he couldn't wait to move onto something more relaxing.

Then I'll find another.

Teddy didn't know what else to do; he had to get Adrian back. Not only for his heart's sake, but for science's sake. Even for the good of all humankind in this world or the next. Who knew what had happened to the universes that ceased to exist, the ones that didn't push or pull through the bridge? Teddy might even be able to stop that from ever happening again if he kept travelling and understanding the nature of the process. He could stop billions of humans snapping out of existence. Surely that was worth the price of one marriage.

And another.

None of this would have been possible without Adrian's brilliant mind, and he had to get it back. Teddy checked the time again knowing he hadn't missed the ninety minute mark, as his stomach would have let him know, but he had to be certain. He went over the plan once more in his head while he waited.

One: Wait until the bridge rotates.

Two: Feel the pull and immediately call Caz and tell the first lie; that he was on the way to Marsh Avenue to check on the bridge, knowing full well it was ready to take him and Adrian.

Three: Phone Caz ten minutes later and tell the second lie, that it had just switched and it was safe for Teddy to cross and he'd need their help to "close the bridge".

Four: Meet them outside the house and quickly enter before they could focus on the feeling too much.

Five: Once inside, the bridge would do the rest of the work.

Caz would be helpless, and Adrian and Teddy could walk through in harmony. No accidents this time. The lore of the bridge would win him over just as it had done the last Adrian. Just as Caz wouldn't be able to stand the push, Adrian wouldn't be able to resist the pull in such close proximity. They wouldn't be using the alley as Teddy had been.

Perhaps Caz would be happier without Adrian too? Teddy wouldn't be around to find out how her story ended. He let his mind wander once more, to a place where he and

Adrian were reunited, jumping from universe to universe. This time with the knowledge that they would always be safe. No slip ups, no dead bodies. As it was meant to be: side by side, through infinity, through eternity.

Teddy shivered at the thought, allowing it to ooze from his cerebellum over his shoulders and down his back. It felt good. It felt joyous. It felt euphoric.

It's calling.

Teddy brought his senses back to the alley and checked the time, although he already knew the ninety minutes had passed. There was no nausea in his stomach now, only desire. He unlocked the phone, his fingers shaking with excitement as he went to set the wheels in motion. Knowledge was certainly power, Teddy thought again.

'Soon,' he said once more, with the wicked smile of eternity painted on his face.

40

Bola hung up his private phone. Adrian and Caz had just phoned. If Bola wanted the killer, he had to leave now.

This is nuts.

They must be having him on; it sounded like time travel. He had been fighting with the idea of telling Kim, but now it was too late. If more people were about to disappear into thin air it made no difference.

Parallel universes.

His hand reached around to his kidney that served as a reminder to trust no one but himself. But he *did* trust himself. After leaving Adrian and Mona, he'd returned to the station and perused over the report and the photos. He would have dug up the body if he had time, but he didn't need to. There was no doubt there were two Adrians. Not a twin, not a doppelganger. Two Adrians.

Bola looked out to sea. It sat eerily still in front of him, offering no answers, the waves barely perceptible in the dusk. He had to get across to Marsh Avenue while everyone was leaving work. He had to arrest this Teddy character, clean up the mess he'd got himself into, and deal with the consequences.

Move!

Bola trudged up the stone shore to the promenade, his buckled shoes slipping about and collecting chalk as they always did. He broke into a jog as the stones thinned out, and was slightly out of breath by the time he sat in the driver seat of his car. He jammed the keys into the ignition, clicked the engine into life and pulled away without so much as a glance in his mirror.

A few roads into town and he was already hitting the end of day traffic. Vehicles of all sizes blocked the narrow streets while pedestrians snaked in and out of the cars, adding to the sense of gridlock. Bola flicked on his private lights and sirens, immediately causing more commotion and stopping dead a pedestrian who was about to jog across the road. He still enjoyed the power of a few blue lights and a god-awful wailing siren after all these years.

Slowly but surely, the traffic began to part down the middle. He began calculating the fastest routes up to Marsh Avenue. He should be there in about ten mins - if the crossings were up. Closer to twenty if he took the bridge. He didn't know how long he had until whatever happened, happened, but he shouldn't have been down on the seafront.

Stupid idea.

He begrudgingly took a right turn leading him towards the bridge thinking he couldn't risk the crossings being down, but he'd no sooner changed his mind and taken the next left towards the crossings.

Stupid idea.

He brought the gears down, engine whining. Within a

couple of minutes, he was on Station Road and seconds away from finding out whether his gut had been playing a trick on him.

The crossings were up.

'Oh, thank fuck.'

He saw traffic up ahead, but nothing he couldn't cut through. Bola gave his sirens an accompaniment with the horn in order to shift the traffic faster, but when he stopped beeping he heard additional sirens in the air. Up ahead, the crossing's beacons had begun to flash and soon enough the first pair of gates began to drop.

'Fuck, fuck, fuck!'

He pulled out into the right lane, dominating the road. He could see the panic from the oncoming vehicles. Police sirens *and* crossing sirens – this was too much for the average driver. Car continued to veer off, but the closer he got, the less kerb there was for drivers to mount. The barriers were dropping at an agonising pace, teasing him.

One more car to go, nearly there.

After a hefty white van scooched aside with the grace of a ballerina, he was met with a battered hatchback, a peach fuzzed teenage boy behind the wheel and a whopping great P plate on the bonnet. The boy stopped dead in the middle of the oncoming lane. Fear was freshly painted on his face and it appeared to be a long way from drying off. They locked eyes. Seeming to sense the gravity of Bola's task, the boy nodded in understanding and visually began reciting what were probably instructions from the book of *Situations you might find yourself in when driving in the real world: Part 1.*

The boy clunked his car into the unmistakable sound of reverse, looked over his shoulder, and began reversing down the road, the little car screaming worryingly as it went. Bola couldn't believe his luck; this kid deserved those P plates. There was no pavement but a tiny sloped driveway for a storefront up ahead and Bola presumed this was the boy's intended target.

Bola looked back to the crossing and the first opposing pairs had come to rest on the ground, blocking Bola's left lane of travel, and oncoming traffic. He still had time before the final pair got moving and touched down. As the drive approached, the boy began feeding the wheel though his hands like a length of rope, perfectly threading the little car up onto the sloped driveway. Bola shook himself out of this astonishment just as the second set of barriers began their descent. He raced forward. As he approached, he gave the boy a quick nod in appreciation of his precision driving, but something wasn't quite right with the physics.

The boy's face was getting closer, and closer. His smile began to falter as he also realised what was happening. The slight gradient was taking him back down the driveway on a crash course.

He hasn't put the handbrake on!

Bola heard a roar from the little engine. It cut through the symphony of sirens just as he was passing, and he knew what it meant. The boy had gone to slam on the breaks and got nothing but the accelerator and a neutral gear. The car rolled down the slope. Its driver was now way beyond any book he'd read in preparation for his test. Gravity did its thing. Bola had nearly cleared the driveway but wasn't moving fast enough. There was a thud from behind and it was enough to shoot the front end of Bola's car offline and into the protective pollard of the crossings.

Bola slammed his brakes on without missing and brought his car to a stop.

The barriers came clattering down and continued to shake, mocking him further as if they were in a fit of giggles. His mind raced ahead and immediately started to estimate the strength of the barriers. Could his radiator and block take that assault? He still had to get up to Marsh Avenue. And what about the inbound train?

Fuck the train!

He shifted his car into reverse and backed up as much as he could. Putting the car into first once more, Bola revved the needle up to four-thousand and dumped the clutch. His car shot forward with a squeal. A crowd of onlookers at the gate started waving their arms wildly. At the very last minute he saw something he wouldn't be able to break through: the dappled lights of a train flashing through the hoardings. Had it been daytime, he might not have seen it. He slammed on his brakes once more and brought his car juddering to a halt, this time careering into the bottom of the gates with just enough momentum to set off his airbags. The world suddenly went dark, then bright powdery white. He kept his eyes closed as he heard the train passing and cursed himself for his stupidity.

41

Adrian and Caz pulled up outside 33 Marsh Avenue and turned off the engine. Something about the dying engine gave Adrian a stir under his skin, like it might not be the only thing that puffed its last breath that day. He tried to push this thought away, not quite knowing where it had come from. The daytime excursion was clearly overwhelming him. Being cooped up had left its mark. The grave thought gave a little resistance then faded away leaving the silence that was in the car. He heard a slither to his side and saw Caz's hand reaching across the handbrake in search of his own. He took it and immediately noticed it was clammy. He brought his other hand across to hers and clasped it tightly.

'It's going to be alright,' he said to Caz. 'There's really no need for you to come in. He might only need one of us anyway.'

'I'll be fine,' Caz said, followed by a burp.

'It's making you sick isn't it? Like it did with that estate agent? Look, there's really no need. Teddy said it was clear for him, not us, and the detective will be here soon.'

'Adrian.' Caz looked him dead in the eye, and for the second time in five minutes, he felt his skin stir once more. 'We need to keep Teddy in there.' She looked at the house. 'That detective *needs* to see this. If not, we have no evidence.'

Teddy was of course unaware there would be an extra guest to witness his departure from this world. Frankly, the risks Teddy had taken were enough to show his worthiness, and the fact he'd made contact with Adrian and Caz at all was an unnecessary risk. He could have found some other unwitting locals, perhaps even some science nuts who would join him. They were only a smidge wiser to these cosmic goings than anyone else in this universe. Why didn't he pop to some universities and pick another scientist instead?

Yes, why indeed?

Again, Adrian pushed the intrusive thoughts away. It was just his OCD ramping up. He looked out the window at the house and slowly shook his head. He couldn't believe such a lovely collection of bricks held a secret so powerful and dangerous. Once the return journey was made, the bridge would seal itself. If what Teddy said held true, and Adrian believed he did. Circuit complete, out of gas, thank you very much

Teddy had said he'd run them through closing the gate, and it was simple enough. They didn't have to *understand* it. He caught some movement in his peripherals and saw someone coming up the street. It was Teddy. He had a rucksack slung across his front, and as he got closer, Adrian also realised he had one on his back. Teddy was clasping the straps of both like a schoolboy.

'Should we be parked directly outside?' Adrian thought aloud.

'It'll help Bola,' Caz calmly replied. 'Let's be honest, we've never been good at sneaking around, and the neighbours probably know us by now. They might think we're the buyers, and Teddy's key will make for a very trustworthy entrance.'

Adrian gave Caz's hand one last squeeze, smiled and slid out of the car.

He seemed to have left his guts in the passenger seat as his feet found the pavement. Teddy glanced at Adrian as he passed by. He had an odd smile on his face, but gave nothing more than a nod on seeing Adrian. He made his way straight up the garden path and into the house before they had even made it halfway up the drive.

'Well,' Caz said. 'Rude.'

Adrian tried to laugh, but couldn't help but think his gut was trying to tell him something. The stirring skin, Teddy's aloof arrival. Perhaps it was just the bridge affecting him. Teddy had said it affected everyone differently. Adrian had only been here once before and he'd never felt sick, just that light tug at the back of his mind. He tried to listen to his body as he made his way up the drive. Were those butterflies in his gut? He looked across to Caz to see how she was, but her resolve must have hardened at the sight of Teddy. They stepped into the house. That's where it all started to change.

After closing the front door, Caz's hand became extra clammy, and instead of reassuring her, Adrian let it slip out of his hand. He kept walking to the room directly ahead. It felt like something was calling him but he didn't quite understand what language it was talking. He heard a stumble behind him and a little thud.

'Adrian,' Caz said from behind. 'Adrian!'

He looked over his shoulder as he continued walking forward. He saw Caz on all fours. Caz reached out a hand to him but her other arm gave way and she crashed to the floor. Adrian laughed at this and continued into the room. With blood thumping in his ears, he pushed the door open. Shortly afterwards, he also found himself on the floor, but more dignified. He looked down and realised he was kneeling. He felt good – better than he had done in years. He tried to focus on the calling sensation and pinned it to the TV. Teddy was looking at with his arms wide, like he was embracing something and receiving something very pleasant in return. As if knowing Adrian was staring like a little boy who was watching something he shouldn't be, Teddy turned around and gave him an almighty smile – a smile so big and toothy, a sane part of Adrian twitched for just a moment, but then he felt his own face morph into a similar state. Then, Teddy spoke, his words massaging Adrian's ears.

'Adrian, I've seen you without this woman in my universe.' Teddy's voice was commanding, yet marred with fresh bleeding from recently closed scars. 'You were so happy. A different man. Free. Free to think like I've never seen anyone think before. You're a genius Adrian. Don't you see that? You and I, we can't only rule the world, we can rule them all. Just us and us alone. I know the signs now; it will always be safe. Think of the worlds we'll see!'

Adrian felt himself nodding in agreement but it was as

if the smile was leading him on, yanking his head up and down. Wonderful worlds, flying cars, alien canteen owners.

'You've been reading my notes, yes? I know they've grabbed you, sparked something you haven't felt in a long, long time. The blind wonder of a child. The notion that you're invincible and nothing is impossible. You can live that again, every day. You can feel what you're feeling now, forever. Come with me.'

Adrian couldn't argue with that; it sounded like a solid plan. He was intrigued. Hell, he was fascinated by what was going on. Yet, when he opened his mouth, he didn't say what he thought he would say. 'You... you did this on purpose?'

The words seemed to hurt Teddy. Everything but his smile faltered.

'Me? No Adrian, it wasn't me. It was something much greater that pulled you here. Leave that woman behind. She'll be fine here without you. As soon as we pass through, her suffering will end, just as yours did.' Adrian did think that was best. Caz hadn't looked well. Again, some remnants of sanity were pulling at Adrian like a child trying to get its parent's attention, but he managed to brush it away one more time. Adrian found his strength and stood. There were no moans of protest from his normally vocal knees. He felt incredible, like he could lift up a car if he wanted to. He started to look around the room for things to lift up and spotted the sofa. Teddy cottoned on seeming to read his mind.

'Yes, yes,' he cried. 'Now you're getting it. You feel the power the cosmos possesses. With my knowledge and your mind, we can harvest this, Adrian. We can make it all ours.'

'All ours?'

That did it. Adrian was sold. His brain was done packing its bags, and that internal struggle had received a final boot into the gutter. He walked towards Teddy and the future that awaited him.

'You fucking piece of shit,' someone said from behind them.

Adrian saw astonishment in Teddy's eyes and he turned around once more to see Caz. She was at the living room door and had propped herself up against it, one hand supporting her and the other wielding not her trusty screwdriver or hammer, but a kitchen knife. A mess of sodden hair hung over her face, her mouth was covered in vomit, and fresh blood poured out of her nose. She didn't look well, but she looked determined and she looked furious.

'I fucking knew you were no good from the moment you stepped into our house.'

'You see Adrian,' Teddy said, ignoring Caz. 'She's absolutely vile. She's narrow minded, constricting you, stifling your potential – *our* potential.'

'You are the vile one here, Teddy. You want Adrian only for the research. You don't love him, you don't *want* him. You're just using him.'

Adrian wasn't entirely sure what they were arguing about, but he knew he should be on Teddy's side so he chimed in. 'That's not true.' The words left his mouth but they didn't feel right, they felt alien. Caz shot him a look.

She has beautiful eyes.

'You're not thinking straight, Adrian. The bridge is pulling you. Teddy lied about its–'

Before she could finish the sentence, she doubled over and heaved bile across the room. Had it not been for the door frame, Adrian thought she would have ended up on the floor again, but Caz held on fast, and instead of resting, she pushed herself away from her support and made for Teddy. Adrian was in awe. He didn't quite know how he knew, but the effort Caz must have exerted to get closer to the bridge was phenomenal. She staggered across the room towards Teddy, fighting against the force of the bridge, brandishing the knife as if cutting a path for herself. That little tug crawled out the gutter and returned to Adrian's side. For the briefest of moments he thought he should help Caz. He went to speak but the smile on his face grew stronger and prevented him from doing so. He looked to Teddy helplessly, and he also saw recognition on his face of this incredible feat – that someone undergoing the push was surging vigorously against it like a Blitzkrieg assault. Only this assault wasn't being made by armoured vehicles, it was being made by a soft, fleshy human body – an army of one against what must have felt like the entire force of the universe.

Caz's legs faltered, then something in her left ankle went. The sound filled the room like a gunshot. On her next step, the knee went in her other leg. In his enlightened state, Adrian understood this instantly as the universe trying to protect Caz from certain doom if she was to cross into the world on the other side of the bridge. A world where another Caz Turner already existed. Caz fell face first trying to stop herself with her arms but she didn't release her grip on the knife. Adrian saw a little fountain of blood splatter between the shoulder blades of his wife, giving way to a few inches of steel that stood proud from her back. Her ankle gave a twitch or two then ceased its Spandau Ballet. A pool of blood surged away from the steel point like lava, burning everything in a deep red as it went.

Adrian didn't need to be a scientist to understand what had happened, the tugging at his side gave one last almighty pull and it felt like an iron veil had been lifted off his senses.

'Caz,' he shouted from the bottom of his soul. Adrian suddenly became aware of his surroundings, the situation and his wife: his beautiful, beautiful wife. He made towards Caz but his body made one last diversion on account of a laugh that filled his ears: it was Teddy. He was standing next to the bridge, laughing at the scene, that awful terrifying smile stuck to his face. A smile that briefly parted and spat onto the body of his wife.

Adrian felt nothing in that moment but raging hot anger. His skin prickled, his pores expanding like a mechanical venting system to try and regulate the absolute inferno of hatred that ran through his body. His final detour was to Teddy, to knock that stupid smile off his fucking face once and for all. He wanted to plant his fist through it and feel the back of Teddy's skull on his knuckles. And so he did. In two steps he felt the squishy flesh under his hot fist, felt the resistance of a jaw and then a little give. It felt marvellous, but he had to get back to Caz.

Caz...

Adrian felt a tug at his side and looked down to see that Teddy had grabbed his shirt in his devilish little hands, pulling Adrian closer, the momentum of his punch still sending most of his body weight forward. He felt his rear foot leave the safety of the floor, leaving him tilting on his planted forward foot, then a moment later that anchor had also gone and he was nothing but a floating mass of hot blood and bones. He waited for the crash of the wall but it never came, for Teddy had shifted his weight around and led them straight into the mouth of the bridge. Adrian looked down at Teddy's face as they fell for what felt like forever, and saw that bloodied smile. A smile that had haunted his dreams before he knew what it was, that had promised him the world and more, a smile as old as the universe itself.

42

Bola saw Caz's car parked up ahead. It was blissfully unaware that its owners were involved in some cosmic crime far beyond the understanding of its little three-cylinder brain. It had one job to do when the key slid in the ignition – to get from A to B without incident– and evidently it had had a more successful journey than Bola and his car. Bola pumped the brakes as he approached and turned his car straight into the drive of 33 Marsh Avenue.

By the time his feet hit the driveway, he knew he was too late. No feeling of sickness had scuttled up his leg and flopped into his gut to push or pull him as Adrian had described. That was the odd feeling he could never quite place on the night he was called here. Perhaps he was too late to find and catch Teddy. But he was suddenly worried about what he *would* find.

He ran up the driveway half crouched, as if expecting bullets to come sailing out the house, but all was quiet. He hammered the closed front door with both of his fists.

'Adrian,' he shouted. 'Caz.' He looked through the

sliver of glass on the door. He saw no shadows and heard no noises from inside the house. Swiftly recalling the layout of the house, he ran off to the wooden gate that allowed access to the rear. He tried the latch but it was also locked. He gave the gate a good shoulder barge and shouted out once more.

'Police. Police. Open this gate.' He eyed up climbing the gate but the timber beam across the top was capped with spikes. He tried to remember what the neighbour's fencing was like. He recalled the height, but was it spiked? Bola hadn't planned to stay and watch any theatrics. This was meant to be a straight arrest without much fuss, but he was late. As time ticked on, he began to swallow the bitter truth that he might have fucked up in trying to take this on alone. Fucked up, just as Adrian and Caz had by keeping it quiet.

'Merde,' he said, kicking the gate. He ran his hands over his face and tried to take a full breath in to compose his thoughts but panic had already begun winding its tendrils around his lungs. He had to get into that house, and he needed help.

Call Kim.

He ran back to his car, hopped in the driver seat and clicked his radio on. As it loaded up, his mind raced through the various tribunals and hearings he might now have to face due to his actions.

'Fuuuuuuuck!' He thudded the dash A beep issued from his radio and the end of some other officer's sentence came through – something about a traffic incident on the bypass. It absolutely dwarfed in scale to the immensity of what could be going on inside that house. He collected his radio and went to call it in. He clicked open the channel but no words came out. He let it click off again.

Bola's eyes had fixed on the section of wooden fencing between the gate and property boundary at the top of the drive. It was pretty much the width of his car. Without being too aware of his actions, Bola closed his door, tossed the radio onto the passenger seat and started up his car.

What's another ding?

He chucked it into first and shot the car up the drive much faster than he intended. He winced away from the windshield knowing he had no airbags to protect him, just as the first sounds of splintering wood met his ears - but he was wrong on the airbag front. There was a pop to his side, and previously undeployed airbags burst into life. The shock made him push the accelerator a moment more in panic before he had the sense to put both feet onto the brake pedal and bring the car to another juddering stop.

After wrestling the deflated airbags that issued from areas of the car he didn't know had them, Bola pulled himself from his write-off and made his way into the garden. He shouted aloud one final time, more so to check that all his parts were still working - the fencing had put up more of a fight than he'd anticipated.

Bola turned the corner and gave the garden a quick once-over before focusing his attention on the doors he knew led into the living room. No one had come running out after his dramatic entrance. His heart thudded in his throat, using his uvula as a speed bag. He was fuming with himself. He'd got onto this rickety roller coaster, alone, with no seatbelt, and had thrust his arms up high, even though all the signs had told him not to. If someone popped their head out of those patio doors, Bola would send their head flying back in with an almighty hook. He clenched his fist and gritted his teeth at the thought, daring someone to do so.

Bola would have a lot of explaining to do, regardless. Even if what he had been told was true, there was also the possibility he would have no evidence to go off. He could sound like a complete maniac. No head appeared. Only frightened voices floating over the neighbouring fences with a backdrop of sirens that met his hot ears.

Bola reached the back door and looked in, his fist still cocked. The remaining sunlight struggled to illuminate the room as it fought with the tall conifers behind. Bola could just make out the scene, and it gave him an enormous sense of déjà vu. Everything looked the way it had done the first time he'd stepped into 33 Marsh Avenue. The picture frames dotted around the room, the sofas and armchairs, all focusing in the direction of the TV - but really, they were focusing on another feature. A dead body lying in the centre of the room. But where Adrian Hoarding had been, now lay the body of his wife, Caz Turner.

ACKNOWLEDGMENTS

Thanks to my wife for the encouragement after finding out that I was writing in secret. Thank you to Colonel Mustard to answering my police enquiries. Thank you to all the proof-readers for lending me your eyes. As always, shout out to Mike for the beautiful cover art.

Most importantly, I'd like to acknowledge you, the reader. Thank you so much for reading, I really do hope you enjoyed it. If you have a moment, please do leave a review on the book's Amazon page. If you liked this book, you'll most likely enjoy my others as well. Go on, treat yourself.

ABOUT THE AUTHOR

Massimo Paradiso is a short-form producer, loud drummer and the author of three novels. Each have staggeringly sold at least one copy. He lives in Sussex with his wife and daughter.

massimoparadiso.com

Printed in Great Britain
by Amazon

46524997R00158